UNSINKABLE

ADVENTURES FROM THE 1910s

DANIELLE ANYANWU

Adventures From The 1910s
Unsinkable

By Danielle Anyanwu.

Faunteewrites Books.

Published by Faunteewrites Limited, Royal Arsenal gatehouse,
London SE18 6AR, England
fauntee.co.uk © 2021.

British Library Cataloguing in Publication Data.
A CIP catalogue record for this book is available from the British
Library.

ISBN: 978-1-913103-03-3

Dedication

- **To My Primary 4 Teacher, Mr Moore, for being a great teacher and making me have interest in historic events.**
- **To my mum and Dad for their love, support and direction.**
- **To my big sister, Chelsea for being an inspiration.**
- **To my younger sister, Jidechi and my baby brother, David for not being annoying.**

**Even God
couldn't sink
this ship."**

UNSINKABLE

BY

DANIELLE ANYANWU.

CHAPTER 1

It was the 10th of April, 1912, a pleasant day on a blooming spring, and Isabella, James, Mother and Father are travelling to America. Mother and Father believe they are going to have a remarkable life in the United States, mainly so James (the oldest child) can have a better opportunity to grow a business. Father is also building a ballet studio in America. However, Isabella wasn't approving of the idea.

"I don't want to go to America, Mother and Father!" Hollered Isabella as she grabbed her big blue velvet pillow. "I need to remain here in England, permanently. America sounds soooooooooo boring!!" Mother and Father didn't answer. Instead, they gave her a ticked off look.

"What if the ship sinks and we all perish? So there's no point going in the first place. England's good enough we don't need to go to America! And... we'll do nothing on the ship." Isabella moaned, sounding like a dejected baby, wishing her parents would change their minds.

"Didn't you hear the news, Isabella? Titanic is unsinkable, and it's true! Who wouldn't want to live the American dream? Here are the newspapers that say so," explained Father half happy, half annoyed, as he patted Isabella lightly on the back.

"That's the only, stupid proof you've got to show the ship won't sink," moaned Isabella.
"No need to include the horrible attitude," Father later mentioned.
"And you still don't have a choice! We have already paid for it. You know that there's hardly any boarding or high-quality schools around here," added Mother, obviously not interested in Isabella's whining. "But what about Anastasia, my best friend? She would be more than devastated if I left her without even telling her! Mother and Father, don't you all understand a word I'm saying?" Isabella yelled, as she swiftly sat up from her comfy bed. "Well, sorry, Isabella, I do not understand." Mother said.

"Well, I do understand," Father said. Mother shot him the ugliest look she's got, and Father kept silent.

"You'll make new friends; probably ones who don't throw their things around their classrooms," Mother replied to Isabella. She mumbled something and laid back on her bed.
"Why are you morons not allowing me to make a decision of where I want to live?" she muttered, but no one heard.

James was in his bedroom, gathering his stuff into his suitcase; acknowledging the sight of the delightful morning sun and people going to the harbour, where the Titanic will arrive. It will then depart and sail to Cherbourg in France then Queenstown in Wales before heading west to New York City.

"It's eternally perfect when you are far, far away from your bothersome parents," James mumbled to himself.

The silence continued, and he began to pack up.

10 seconds later, James overheard some rambling across the hallway to Isabella's room. He scurried his feet through the hall and to Isabella's bedroom, where all the commotion was coming from. James kicked open Isabella's door to see both his parents whining at Isabella, but he didn't mind.

"What's the matter?" James asked, trying to sound concerned by the whole situation, but he didn't care at all. His mother, still feeling bitter about the situation, answered, "Your sister doesn't want to go to America." Isabella turned her head to the other side of the bed.
"Mother, you have to start getting used to how stuck up Isabella is," James said.
"I'm not stuck up! You are. That's why you have no friends," Isabella jeered. "Shut up, Isabella!" James spat back rudely. "Shut up, James!" Isabella shouted again.
"Now, you two stop whining like idiots," Mother screamed, "You don't have a choice Isabella! So dress up this instant!"

"Isabella, you're kinda crazy, really, who wouldn't want to go to America?" James asked.

"Me!" Isabella snapped.

"You must learn to start accepting changes," James said.

"What a nuisance!" Isabella remarked.

"Let me see how 'rubbish' this ship is," James muttered:

"The RMS Titanic is the biggest ship ever to be built, carrying 2,224 passengers and crew members. The boat will also be boarded by some of the wealthiest people in the world, as well as emigrants from Great Britain, Ireland and Scandinavia. The ship will enter service and will be the second of the three Olympic ocean liners, operated by the White Star Line. She is built by Harland and Wolff who have said in Ireland that it is unsinkable. The Captain of the ship is Edward John Smith; it will be his final journey on the Titanic before his retirement."

James read that statement as quickly as he could, and once he was finished, he breathed like a bulldog. "I shouldn't have read it so fast," said James, and he fell on Isabella's armchair.

The chair was comfy with lavenders near the bottom of the chair and had a velvet mauve colour cushion. In front of the chair was a redwood dresser; and inside the drawers were full of nicely kept earrings, necklaces, rings, bracelets, ornaments, bangles and pieces of crystals and diamonds, latest perfumes, gloves, socks, hair accessories and Isabella's diamond rhinestone piggy bank. Inside the piggy bank was £1,500 that Isabella had saved up.

Isabella's diamonds, rubies, emeralds and aquamarine jewellery and so on, were inside a big safe that was moveable in her luggage. Those were Isabella's favourite things that Mother and Father had bought her. She had two turquoise necklaces with thin golden linen at the middle of the pendants. So she gave her other one to Anastasia as a friendship necklace.

"See, Isabella, going on the Titanic won't be so crazy," said Father. Isabella still rejected the persuasion. Isabella absolutely didn't want to leave England; she wanted to stay with Anastasia, her best friend forever! She would miss her school and her classmates, including her home and bedroom. This all seemed not so fair to her in any manner.

After hours of whining, Mother finally convinced Isabella to go, "I'm only going because I don't want to live alone as a girl," Isabella replied.

"Don't worry, Isabella. I'll help you wear the best dresses in your bureau," Mother said. That wasn't what was worrying Isabella. She went out of the bed and removed her hair tie; her brown, wavy hair came all out in an instant. "I'll go run you a bath, Isabella. Start removing your clothes; and when you are done bathing, put on some cream and wear your robe. Call me so I can arrange your hairstyle and get you a sophisticated dress. I'll be in the Not-Quite-Sure-What-To-Call-It-But-Do-Whatever-You-Want-Because-We're- Not-Bothered-To-Give-It-A-Proper-Name room, okay; I should've said, N, Q, S, W, T, C, I, B, D, W, E, Y, W, B, W, N, B, T, G, I, A, P, N. But that's too long to remember so I should've said, 'spare room or lounging room'." Mother said. Isabella didn't respond; she ran to her dresser and brought out her pendant, the friendship pendant. She held it for some time, then she stared at the turquoise necklace. She took the pendant as she strolled to the dusty lavender window seat and looked out of the window. The streets outside were not too dark, and there were many people in their cars and outside; "Probably to see Titanic depart or that they're going to be passengers." Isabella thought. She heard the water running in the bath in the bathroom, and James complained so someone could bring his towel all the way from here.

Mother came back in the room and told Isabella, "You can have your bath now; don't go into James's room because he's dressing up," and she disappeared downstairs into the Not-Quite-Sure-What-To-Call-It-But-Do-Whatever-You-Want-Because-We're-Not- Bothered-To-Give-It-A-Proper-Name room.

Isabella got her towel from her closet and walked into the bathroom. She was confused that Mother put her doll, Lotta Spring in the water because now it was bobbing up and down like a dead, drowned baby. Isabella stared at the thing in horror, "Lotta Spring, did Mother put you in the water?" Isabella asked. Lotta Spring didn't answer, she continued to bob up and down in the hot water. Isabella then tossed Lotta Spring out of the bathroom and it made a big THUD on the carpet.

She heard James opening his bedroom door and screamed frantically.
"There's a dead thing in front of me!!" James shrieked. She heard his feet jumping up and down since he was screaming like a lunatic. Isabella then heard Mother and Father running upstairs and telling him that it's just Lotta Spring, Isabella's doll. Mother said she dropped her into the water then Isabella probably threw her out of the bathroom.
She heard James and Father laughing to themselves, plus she overheard Father saying how silly he was and James telling him to shut up and Mother saying not to use lousy language to Father. And they went into the Not-Quite-Sure-What-To-Call-It-But-Do -Whatever-You-Want-Because-We're-Not-Bothered-To-Give-It-A-Proper-Name room across the hall from the parlour downstairs. Isabella giggled and began to wash herself as she ran lots of more water from the tap .

After throwing Lotta Spring in front of James's, eavesdropping on Father, Mother and James and bathing, Isabella ran into her bedroom and put cream on herself. She closed the blue blinds and put on her silk pink and green blossom printed robe on. Isabella shouted to Mother to come here and do her hair.

Mother tiredly came upstairs as if it was night time. She was wearing a white and black morning suit. A big beautiful green embroidery was in the middle of her black silk dress. She had on a black picture hat with white flowers and feathers sticking out of it. She was wearing light mesh gloves that were up to her wrist. The necklace Mother was wearing was a royal blue gem shaped like a sphere, and she had a teardrop formed cerulean earring. Mother carried a black lace parasol, and on the other hand, she held a walking white silk purse that had a black rhinestone in front of it.

"Let's arrange your hair, shall we?" Mother asked Isabella. Isabella nodded her head and got Lotta Spring in her hands, ready to do her hair. Mother pulled out the chair, and Isabella sat in front of the dresser, looking at herself in the mirror. Mother got out a comb and some little silk bows.
"What should it be today, little Isabella?" Mother asked, "Should it be all out, ponytail, bun or french braids?"
"I want a sleek updo," Isabella answered. Mother looked at her in shock.
"Why do you want a sleek updo, that's not what little girls like you wear, and it's highly unprofessional and absurd!" Mother respond-ed, not happy at all. Isabella didn't say anything. She used her mini hairbrush and began to brush Lotta Spring's little ginger hair.
"Let's give you a braided updo, shall we? We'll add that green flower here, and you'll wear your gloves up to your wrists and your emerald necklace. Make sure NO ONE touches your emerald neck-lace, okay? Great. Now all you need is your dress..." Mother said as she looked around inside Isabella's suitcases for her dress. Mother kicked open a suitcase, but her clothes weren't inside. "For crying out loud!!" Mother mentioned as she poured open another suitcase.

Isabella giggled inside as her mother wasn't being normal. "This is truly ridiculous!" Mother exploded, "With all this luggage on the way, I can't find a single piece of your outfit!" Isabella didn't an-swer or seem to care. She was almost done with Lotta Spring's hair. She tied on a big blue ribbon at the back of Lotta Spring's head. Now all that was left was Lotta Spring's sailor costume.

Mother zipped open a white bag, and Isabella's poison ivy green and white dress were neatly folded inside. Her flat green shoes were tidily next to the green gown and her white cardigan, not to mention her green and white garden hat. "Fantastic!" Mother cheered, "This will all match perfectly! Isabella, wear all this, okay? Wonderful! Splendid!"
Mother walked out of Isabella's bedroom. Isabella put Lotta Spring inside her suitcase and began to dress up.

CHAPTER 2

James was in his bedroom, packing more of his belongings into his suitcases and bags and stuff. He packed his clothes, radio, shoes, paintbrushes and some extra things.

"James, are you finished dressing up?" Father shouted to James from downstairs.
James came out of his room and saw Father still downstairs, waiting for an answer. James went down the stairs, wearing a lower class suit and he didn't even add gel on his hair. Father opened his eyes wide in disgust.

"What on earth are you wearing, James?!" Father asked.
James looked down at his 'suit' and answered, "I'm wearing this! What's so bad about it?" "Sorry, but don't you notice that what you are wearing looks poorer than a broke man's outfit? I mean you didn't even add a little bit of gel on your hair!!" Father shouted. James didn't answer. Mother came and told James and Father, "The people are here to get all our luggage; it's too late for James to change now. Tell Isabella that she has to hurry up now."

Father, James and Mother heard the wagon pulling up in their driveway and Mother thrust the door open. A man in a brown suit and a checkerboard jumped out of the car that was pulling the wagon. He was big, and had scruffy brown hair. Mother readily walked up to the man even though she despised his uncanny look.

"Greetings, Sir, is that the cart you are using to load our luggage?" Mother asked.
The man answered in a foreing accent, "Yes mam, we'll be getting three of your safes, all your clothes and furniture, not to mention all your cutlery and stuff and the rest of your personal things." the man replied, showing her all of the things she agreed to put on the wagon.
"Great! Start packing the things in the living room, kitchen, drawing room, James's bathroom, Family bathroom, Parent bathroom, the Not-Quite-Sure-What-To-Call-It-But- Do-Whatever-You-Want-

Because-We're-Not-Bothered-To-Give-It-A-Proper-Name room-"
Mother said until she was 'rudely' interrupted by the man.
"What is the room you just said? I didn't get that." the man said.
Mother got a paper and a quill and wrote the Not-Quite-Sure-What-
To-Call-It-But-Do-Whatever-You-Want- Because-We're-Not-Bothered-To-Give-It-A-Proper-Name room.
"And that's not all too," Mother said, "We need all our furniture
from the prayer room, entertainment room, hair room, my footwear
room, gym room, study room, children's room, smoking room even
though no one uses it, and that's it!" The man looked at her confus-
ingly. "That's a LOT of rooms!!" The man said.
"I know! Perhaps you and your buddies should begin hurrying up
shall you soon?" Mother replied sweetly and strolled into the man-
sion. The gentlemen in the wagon all sprang out and walked into the
first room; which was the kitchen.

Isabella was in her room, finishing up with Lotta Spring's dress.
"Now you look so better, Lotta Spring!!" Isabella whispered and
stroked Lotta's hair slowly. She heard someone knocking on her
door and assumed it was Mother. "Come in," Isabella called out.
And... suddenly, a group of men opened the door, and Isabella
began to scream. "Who are you, men?!" Isabella asked, looking
frightened as she stood up from her piano stool. "Nothing to worry,
small girl, we just have to collect all your belongings and put them
in a wagon in front of the house. Your family is going on the Titanic, right?" one of the men asked. Isabella didn't say anything, she
just nodded her head.

"Put your freakish dolly inside one of your suitcases and leave so
we can start to do our process," the man rudely pointed out. Isabella
picked up Lotta Spring and put her inside her silk green and white
bag with a golden handle and an image of a green leaf. She took
her bag and walked out of her bedroom, wishing that she told the
men to get lost.

CHAPTER 3

Isabella waltzed to James where he was sitting in the garden and looking at the pond.

"Greetings, James, what are you doing looking in the garden?" Isabella asked.

"I was running away from Father! He wanted to add gel on my hair, and I DESPISE gel!" James groaned, not looking at Isabella who got Lotta Spring out from her green and white bag. Isabella sighed and sat next to James, looking at the water. He turned to Isabella and saw her looking sad.

"What is the matter, Isabella?" James asked.

Isabella sighed again and answered, "I am not sure if I'll be able to live without Anastasia! I really don't know what I'm going to do without her! If I could just talk to her for ONE last time, it'll be a beautiful dream!!" Isabella mumbled, lying on the long cold grass. James looked at her with such disgust. "I'm going to miss all the Iris, Blue Delphinium, Forget-Me-Not, Himalayan Blue Poppy, Daisy, Daffodil, Jasmine, Dogwood and Marigold flowers! Remember when Dixie called them skinny flowers?" Isabella chatted. James didn't respond.

After a minute of no talking, James asked Isabella, "You're going to miss Anastasia, aren't you?"

Isabella slowly nodded her head. "I just said it!"

"You should get used to it, you might find a better friend. Once you move on, you'll forget about her," James advised.

A long puff of breeze swept around the rustling green leaves and brown trees; the blue and white flowers moved to the rhythm of the cold wind as the sun was beginning to show it's glow. "It's getting cold! I'll be going inside, come on, Isabella." James said, standing and removing the ruffles on his trousers. Isabella still lay on the grass next to a bunch of Blue Delphinium flowers. "Aren't you coming in? You don't want to get your dress all dirty," James said, opening the door into the drawing-room.

"I'm good here, thank you, since when did you care about how I look?" Isabella said as she held Lotta Spring up in the air.

"Don't know. Suit yourself!" James said, and he closed the door.

Isabella sighed again and closed her eyes.

James sat on a box in the drawing-room. "Ahhh, not cold no more," James sighed as he rubbed his palms together. A man came up to him and said, "You're meant to be removing this furniture! Not resting on 'em!! James looked at the man in shock.
"I'm not one of you! I live here!" James said.
"If you live here, you would've been wearing an upper-class suit!" The man quipped. "Well, I live here! My mother said you lot are doing the work!" James said, giving him a stern look. Father heard James shouting at someone from his bedroom, getting ready. "Goodness," Father muttered as he got his walking stick and his golden pocket watch. "What's all that noise?!" Father asked as Mother came in. She shrugged her shoulders and got her diamond ring from her dresser. "Let's find out what James is whining about." Mother said as she and Father walked downstairs to the drawing-room. "I hate being a parent to him…" Father sighed

"What is the matter, Sir?" Mother asked as she adjusted her hat to the right angle.
"Sorry, but this man is 'apparently' living with you due to the fact he doesn't look rich at all!" The man who was complaining about James said. Mother and Father glared at James, "This is our son, James," Father said. "Oh, I'm very sorry!" the man stuttered embarrassingly.
"That's okay, fine man, sometimes I tell James not to wear such clothes, you can continue removing our stuff now!" Father sarcastically laughed.
"Okay, Sir!" the man said, he glared at James and James glared at him back and he walked away with a piece of luggage.
"That is what happens if you DON'T wear an upper-class suit, James!" Mother said. James didn't say anything. He was about to walk away, but Father asked, "James, where is Isabella. I didn't see her in her room?"
"She's outside lying in the garden," James answered.
"LYING IN THE GARDEN?!" Mother screamed in horror. James happily nodded, and Mother was quite annoyed.
"She's stupid, isn't she!" James laughed.

"Use your manners, James," Father said as he hit the floor with his walking stick.

"Let me go get that silly Isabella!" Mother said walking out into the garden.

"Isabella, be a good girl, and stop lying on the grass like a silly person!" Mother shouted angrily. Isabella sat up from the grass, a bit startled, and saw Mother walking towards her, opening her parasol.

"Hello, Mother! What are you doing here?" Isabella asked. Mother didn't reply.

"Isabella, get off the grass this instant! You'll get your gown all dirty," Mother said as she pulled Isabella up. Isabella grabbed her white and green hat and her bag from the floor. "Let's get inside," Mother later whispered, now more gently.

CHAPTER 4

After about an hour, the men were all done with putting the family belongings in the wagon (which was kind of quick). The man who first spoke to Mother came out of the carriage and said to Father, "Now since we're done, you have to pay us each 10 shillings, but I and one more person will connect this cart to your car and drive it to where Titanic will depart," Father nodded his head, and once the man was done blabbing, he said, "Thank you for putting our stuff into the carriage and going to take our things to the Titanic, Sir. Bring your men so I can give them... ten shillings," Father said, hating the word shilling because he never talks about a shilling which is a tiny amount of money.
The men all hurried to Father and waited in a line for their shillings. Once they were done, the man sat on top of the cart as Father looked at the sunny sky. "Let's get this journey started!" He happily whispered as his hat shaded the warm sun.

"Whatever," James shouted from upstairs in his room out of the window. Father looked up and saw James smiling and sticking his tongue out. "James, do keep your tongue inside your mouth and get down here! We're going to start going!" Father joyfully shouted, facing James. "Yesssssss! We are going!!" James shouted as he skipped downstairs like those little girls who sing tacky nursery rhymes and go to private preschools. James ran down to the drawing room to Isabella and Mother, screaming out loud, "WE'RE GOING TO AMERICA!"

Mother sprang off the floor and danced around in satisfaction, her jewellery jiggling around. Isabella, on the other hand, did not have a happy expression on her face; in fact, Isabella was petrified.
"What? Now? America? Without Anastasia?" She stuttered as she stood up with Lotta Spring.
"Yes, baby, now!!!!" James shouted, "Let's get lost!!" As he ran out of the door, into the driveway. "Eeeek! I'm so excited! I remember announcing to you we're going on the Titanic in a month, but now we're going NOW!!!" Mother shrieked as she held Isabella by the hand and walked out of the house.

So the family were able to begin their first part of a vacation on the sea. Father waited for everyone to come out of the house, and he locked the door for one last time and put the key under the rug that said: "La douceur du foyer" which meant 'Home sweet home' in French.

"This is going to be sooo, not fun!!!" Isabella said to James. Father went on the car and Mother went to the car that the men were going to drive.

"Don't be like that, silly Isabella; I've heard that they have a gym and astonishing bedrooms." He ruffled Isabella's brown hair. It made Isabella pretty happy.

"Fine," Isabella said. "I'll try to have fun." and she looked at Lotta Spring, waiting for James, who had to fasten his shoelaces.

"Hurry up, James!" Father called out as he sat impatiently on the car. Mother went and sat inside the car.

"You'll be sitting with me," She said, and Isabella nodded her head. "James looks like you'll be sitting out here with me!" Father said again. James didn't answer. He muttered something under his breath as Isabella walked to the car and Mother helped her up. James came out of the car and strolled to Isabella, and whispered to her from the window.

"Have fun," and he disappeared into the passenger seat, next to Father, in front of their car. "Are you buckled up, James? Good, let's start going!" Father cheered and started the keys.

CHAPTER 5

They started to drive behind Father as Isabella sighed to herself as the car drove past Anastasia's house. She remembered how she first met Anastasia sitting on her front door, but now the house looked abandoned. The car slowly drove past the school; Laplokey private primary school, the school she and Anastasia promised each other they'll finish primary school together at and go to secondary school again together, but now Isabella had broken that promise.

The car drove on the road she and Anastasia walked through to the corner shop where they secretly bought sweets. Isabella remembered the day Anastasia screamed when she saw a dog hurrying toward her, and the hound licked her hand. Anastasia and Isabella laughed so hard before they quickly ran home. The dog was named Shepard, and his older brother was named German. They were German Shepherds obviously.

Isabella was going to miss her whole life here in Southampton. A tear ran down her soft cheeks as she drew a sad face on the window with her breath. Mother noticed Isabella sobbing to herself. Mother moved closer to sit next to her. She removed her picture hat and placed it on her lap before she hugged Isabella.
"I know you're sad that you're leaving Southampton to go to America, but you need to move to have a better life. I had to leave Wales to marry your father in London, Isabella," Mother quietly said as she used a handkerchief to wipe the sad face off the window. "You don't want to get the car dirty," Mother quietly said. Isabella didn't say anything.
"But if Anastasia was an excellent friend, she would understand that you have to leave; you'll have good friends like Anastasia; probably even better." Mother later continued to try to calm Isabella as she looked out of the window.
"I can forget Southampton and the school; but not Anastasia," Isabella quietly said as she heard James shout, "TITANIC WILL BE COOL, YO!" then she heard Father telling him to keep his mouth shut, but he continued screaming anyway. "Maybe Titanic will be fun with my family," thought Isabella. That'll be something for her

to find out.

The family arrived at Southampton, at 10:09 am, on time, and the sun was almost up in the middle of the cloudless, sunny and blue sky. There was a health check stand, lots and lots of cars, so many people and so much noise.

"HUNK HUNK HUNK!" James blared Father's horn as many annoying people were in the way. "For crying out loud, can these people MOVE ALONG! I've got a life to live and it's only one!" James shouted.
"Stop it!" Father hissed as James did what he was told. The car stopped and James looked around.
"Ahhhh!" Father quietly said. "The unsinkable ship's right in front of my face!!"
"I'm so excited to meet new people here; mostly the first-class people!" Mother said as the man kindly took her hand helping her to get out of the car. Mother opened her parasol and looked at the Titanic; her royal blue necklace, reflecting on the sunlight.
"Hopefully they'll be rich people you're meeting," James said as he hopped out of the car and looked at the commotion. "Judging by what you're wearing, James, I wouldn't be surprised if any upper-class person won't be talking to you." Mother said under her breath.

Isabella still didn't say anything as the man helped her out of the car. She's never seen so many people in one place before. It was very strange to her. James walked up to Isabella, full of excitement. "The ship's bigger than you thought, huh?" James said to her, as hundreds of passengers walked past them. Isabella didn't say anything, but instead, she smiled and nodded her head quickly.
"Do you wonder where they'll store all of this load?" Isabella asked James. He shrugged his shoulders.
"Probably at the bottom of the ship," He later suggested. Then he rudely burped into a 1st class man's face. "Manners," the man hissed out at James. James didn't seem to care.

"My tummy is a little weird..." Isabella whispered as she leaned on Mother's shoulder. "Don't worry, Isabella, your tummy will be better." Mother said, and she walked to Father and they held each other, pointing and looking at everyone else. The steward asked them what class they're in and Mother told him they're 1st class passengers.

"All our stuff is in this wagon right here!" Father pointed at the carriage behind them.
The steward said, "Okie dokie," and he got some men to help collect most of the luggage.
"Can we start going into the ship now? This crowd of people is making my stomach considerably ill." Isabella moaned.
"Yeah, let's start going in!" said the steward and they began to walk to the front of the ship.
"WAIT!" Father called out as he jumped into the wagon and got his camera. "Photo first!" He smiled as he asked the steward to take a picture of the family. "Everyone, say Titanic!" James sarcastically said. Everyone shouted 'Titanic' and the steward took the photo. That was one of the most decent photos taken without James ruining it. "Now we can start going," Father grinned.
"I'm so excited!!" James said repeatedly as he pushed in front of Isabella and went inside the high gangway.
"Watch where you're walking, James!" Mother said as she looked at the crowd. "I don't care!" James said and he pushed his way to the footbridge.

CHAPTER 6

Isabella walked up the footbridge behind the men who were carrying the luggage that they'll mostly use. A girl with her mother barged into Isabella quite rudely. Isabella thought the girl was Anastasia because she had the same green eyes and the same black hair and the same turquoise pendant Isabella had. She was wearing an ivory dress and had black socks and black Mary Jane shoes. The girl held a white suitcase and had a small black hat.

"May we hurry up, Mother!? The crowd of commotion is bothering me too much..." Anastasia whispered to her mother, covering her ears with her hands.

"Hold yourself together, Anastasia, we are almost there!" her mother bitterly answered as she pulled her up. They were about to pass through until some ticket man stopped them.

"Are you 1st class?" he asked. Anastasia's mother nodded her head.

"Look at the ticket," she said as she shoved the ticket into the man's face.

"What is your name?" the ticket man asked Anastasia and her mother, holding his checkerboard.

"Her name is Anastasia, Edith Jerkisco," Anastasia's mum answered.

"And your name, mam," the ticket man asked Anastasia's mother.

"I'm not coming; I'm only going to help her settle in," she answered. The ticket man nodded his head as Anastasia, her mother, some servants and a steward walked passed him, into the first class hallway.

"When I'm gone, Anastasia, do not talk to strangers, because there are so many idiots of the world here! Don't go into places you don't know, and never go into 2nd and 3rd class. They might not have bathed in days!" Mother said as she kept straightening Anastasia's hair.

"Too many things to do, Mother! I will not remember most of them!"Anastasia whined.

"Well, unfortunate luck, Anastasia, unfortunate luck!" Her mother reaffirmed, spitting on her brutally as she chatted.

"Yes, mother..." Anastasia kept answering to her mother's chattering as she bumped into the steward. The steward opened her bedroom door, and it looked amazing! The place was floral, and the servants forced their way into the room and began to unpack Anastasia's stuff and put them into the cupboards and wardrobes.

"You got a parlour suite, a promenade deck, two bedrooms, a private bathroom and a drawing-room, Miss Jerkisco."
"Is that all for me?!" Anastasia gasped happily. The steward nodded his head. "You're also equipped with a private maid, she'll be coming soon, and her name is Maid Victoria, Miss Jerkisco."
"She goes by the name, Anastasia," her mother pointed out rudely. All Anastasia could do now is hope that Isabella was on the Titanic.

"If you need me, Anastasia, ring this steward bell right here," the steward said helpfully.
 He pointed at a golden bell that was behind the door. "But for now, cheerio!" and he left Anastasia alone with some maids putting her stuff in order. "I wouldn't need to be seeing him any time soon," Anastasia thought to herself as she looked hard on the floor. She began to feel quite weird talking to countless strangers; she's never done that before in her life.

A maid entered Anastasia's room with a blue box full of her notebooks and classic novels like Aunt Jane's Nieces on Vacation, Chronicles of Avonlea, Il Giornalino di Gian Burrasca, The Magic World, Maya the Bee, Phoebe Daring, Sky Island, The Tale of Mr Tod, War of the Buttons.

"Where would you like your books and journals to be placed, Anastasia?" The maid asked. "I want my book collection here, next to my bedroom in this cabinet; don't forget to put my shoes from most formal to informal, please and thank you," She got out her jewellery and put it in a drawer that was made of hardwood.

"Where do you want me to put your tea dresses, gowns, hats, accessories and your nightdress, Miss?" Asked the maid named Victoria. Her hair was really dark brown, and her eyes were brown too. Anastasia looked at her, awkwardly.

"I want them in this wardrobe; ordered by most significant to petite. I also want my accessories in this drawer, ordering from most important to least precious too. Organise the rest of my things any way you want."

"Maid Victoria, you do not have to call me Miss because you are older than I am. So I shall call you Maid or Miss Victoria. You shall call me Anastasia." Anastasia said as she got out a colouring set and put it on a table in the parlour suite, ordering the colours like a rainbow. "Beautiful colour; like a rainbow..." She whispered.
Maid Victoria giggled to herself and answered, "Yes, Anastasia." There was an awkward silence as Anastasia unpacked her stuff and Miss Victoria organised them. This made Anastasia extremely uncomfortable.
Anastasia walked out into the private promenade deck. She sat on the deck chairs for a little bit and looked at the tall green plants. She could not hear as much noise as she could listen to outside where all the crowd was; this made Anastasia very relaxed. "Maybe I could play chess with Isabella if she is here!" Anastasia whispered to herself as she went out of the private promenade deck.

Another maid came into Anastasia's room with a picture of four types of flowers.
"Your mother just wanted to ask you what group of flowers you want that will be in a vase; Allium & Amaryllis or Anemone & Alyssum? By the way, both Anemone & Alyssum are white, and the Allium & Amaryllis are purple."

Anastasia looked at both the pictures with the flowers. "I like the colour white, so I'll go for the white Anemone & the white Alyssum flowers; there are enough purples in this room," she answered.
"Very well," the maid said and walked away. It wasn't long before two servants came with two Anemone & Alyssum flowers in a vase and put them on a table outside on the promenade deck.
"Thank you," Anastasia mumbled, but the men didn't answer.

"Can I walk on the decks outside, Maid, Victoria? She asked.

"Of course, just memorise what bedroom door number you have and don't talk to second and third-class passengers like your mother said, have fun!" Victoria called out, and Anastasia walked out with the keys in her hands. She wrote the door number on her palm with a golden pen and walked away, not even bothering to say hello to anyone who said hello to her.

"Victoria!" Anastasia smiled as she unlocked her bedroom door and sat on the bed. Her mother got out Anastasia's hair set, got the brush and brushed her silky black hair. "Goodness, Anastasia, your hair is so all over the place, can't you keep your hair in order?!!" her Mother said.

"Thank you, Mother, so much!" Anastasia said.

"Don't thank me because you need extravagance as you leave to stay with your father, who I truly hate, I still hate you though, and I've never loved you," her mother whispered in her ears bitterly. Anastasia didn't respond.

Her mother left the room without saying bye to Anastasia.

CHAPTER 7

"Follow me, now!!" the steward said as James was shouting Titanic repetitively.

"Shut up, James! You're making us look like frauds!!" Mother moaned as she fanned herself with her big black, feathered fan.

"Maybe we are frauds," James said. He glared at Mother then kept quiet.

"Are you excited, son?" Father asked, impatiently, "I really can't wait!"

"Yeah, I'm pretty excited too!" James said.

"Here we are, now they're only about two beds, so I don't know how you'll organise yourselves..." the steward said. No one said anything. "Very well, here is your bedroom accompanied by a private maid, Alice, a parlour suite and small private promenade deck and continuing; you've read the article of the newspapers haven't you?"

"A what?! Private maid!? Own promenade deck!? Parlour suite!? My life is amazing" Mother screeched in happiness. "Open the doors, old man! Mamma needs to see a load of this!"

The steward nodded his head, feeling disrespected. He unlocked the doors and the maids all came out of nowhere and started organising the rooms and putting their stuff into wardrobes and cupboards.

"Shall I show you your private promenade?" the steward asked Father.

"Yay Yuh!!" James shouted. The man looked at him, bewildered and said, "Let's start going..."

Mother decided not to come; she saw all the maids and servants helping them put all their stuff in the right places.

"These people are accommodating!" Mother said.

"Whatever that means," Father said, "It's true!"

"This is where I'm gonna play all day like a stupid baby!" James said as he hit the wooden floor like an idiot.

"Stop making noise, James, you're acting like a dog!" Father said.

"Don't you like dogs?!" James asked, laughing.

"Yeah, but not inconvenient and stupid dogs!" Father replied as James got up with Father's black walking stick. "Or maybe you hear something else; there're many dogs here!" James said. Father gave him the stare that means he'll use his cane and slap him into hell. Isabella sorrowfully glanced at herself in the big mirror and kept on sighing. Mother noticed that Isabella hasn't happened to speak to anyone.

"You're not speaking to anyone at all, silly Isabella. What's wrong?" Mother asked as she told her to sit on a sofa personally. "I'm not so happy here without Anastasia, Mother. However, you don't understand. You informed me when I woke up this morning," Isabella muttered to Mother.
"I do understand, Isabella. I understand that you're unhappy that you are not going to live with Anastasia like an everyday thing..." Mother said.

There was a tense silence.

"Maybe when we get to America, we can phone Anastasia? What do you say?!" Mother asked. Isabella smiled up at Mother then and said, "That'll be fantastic, Mother; thank you." They hugged each other and Mother told her to run along and see the private promenade.
"Fashionable place!" Father said to the steward. "Get a long table here so that my wife can have tea parties with her friends. Decorate it with flowers and a little velvet blanket in the corner so that Isabella can play with her little dolls and stuff," Father said.
"Very well," the steward said and was about to leave.
"Why does EVERY steward or maid say, 'Vey well?" James asked, mimicking the steward's voice. The steward wanted to slap him into Egypt.
"When's that private maid coming?" Mother promptly asked as she added lipstick on her mouth. "She'll be coming soon; and by the way, her name is Alice. Mind you, she can be very confident about what she thinks..." said the steward. The steward closed the door and left.

"AAAAAAAAAAAAAHHHHHHHHHHH!!!" James screamed in relief once the man was gone for no particular reason.

"What was that for?!" Father asked.

James shrugged his shoulders. "I just wanted to let out some energy, you know!" James laughed.

"Very well," Father whispered as he looked at his pocket watch like a reasonable person. "Stop saying that!!!" James said loudly.

CHAPTER 8

Isabella got out some pots of paint and paper from James's suitcase and was about to draw in the private promenade before she thought of something else.

"Mother, can I go and have a walk around the decks, please?" Isabella asked. Mother didn't say anything at all. She just looked dumbly at the floor like someone with problems. Mother didn't listen to what Isabella said.

"I see why that wouldn't be a bad idea; let's all go. The ship will be leaving soon!" Father said.

"You gotta be kidding me?!" James whined.

"I'm not kidding you; I am adulting you, so let's start going!" Father laughed and stopped as quickly. James rolled his eyes, got his jacket from the suitcase and left.

"What did we just agree to?" Mother asked as she stopped fanning herself and jumped off the sofa.

"We're going to walk in the decks, Mother." Isabella said smiling as she put Lotta Spring in her bag because before she was dead-like on the floor. Mother and Father hurried behind James, who was probably annoying a stranger. Isabella decided to put on some cream on her face and a green bonnet in case it was hot outside. She looked out of the window, but the ship wasn't moving. She put on her white silk gloves and strolled out of the bedroom.

She walked slowly down the hallway, to the entrance so she could ask for directions. Her family didn't wait for her, so she needed to know where to go. As the men opened the door for her and she went down the wooden staircase, she noticed that the identical girl she saw before with black hair and green eyes looked a lot like Anastasia Jerkisco, her autistic best friend. She was sitting on the staircase, putting her hands on her ears. Isabella gazed closer to the girl as she sat on the stairs. She realised it was Anastasia; such shock came upon her face.

Isabella knew that it'd be better to ask her if she was Anastasia, so she didn't decide to shout her name. She walked behind Anastasia. She was moving around the stairs a little fast.

"Are you Anastasia?" Isabella asked as she tapped her on the
shoulder. Anastasia didn't answer, instead she stared at Isabella. She
felt a lot more awkward how Anastasia stared at her face. Anastasia
then recognised Isabella and immediately began to chat excitedly.
"Greetings, Isabella, Doris, Norflook, I can't believe you're here,"
Anastasia smiled. Isabella smiled back, sat on the step next to her
and hugged her.
"Hello, Anastasia. I assumed you weren't coming! I was going
to miss you so much!!!" Isabella explained cheerfully. Anastasia
smiled back at her so much.
"I also assumed you weren't going on the Titanic. The tickets for 1st
class passengers were going to be quite expensive," Anastasia said
as she kneeled down on the floor.

She put her hands in front of her ears.
"Gaaaaa! Noise; don't like it..." she continued to whisper. Isabella
looked down at Anastasia who was rolling around on the floor.
"Are you okay?" Isabella questioned finally as she saw her acting
dead on the ground.
"You don't look too well," Anastasia didn't answer, then she gently
nodded her head as she weakly stood up from the floor.
"I'm good, thank you!" Anastasia later whispered slowly.
"What tickets did you get? I got a 1st class," Anastasia flatly said.
"Sorry, I'm a 3rd class passenger." She replied, looking a little
moody. "JOKE!" yelled Isabella. Anastasia looked at her very con-
fusingly.
"How can I laugh from that; for that it is a lie, and you can't say
sorry because you didn't make me upset and now I don't know if
you are lying or not because this might be all a lie and if you are
not lying, which tickets do you have then?" She asked. Isabella
answered cheerfully,
"I unmistakably have 1st class tickets!" She danced up and down,
squealing like a piglet. Anastasia was still confused but did the same
thing.

"Where is your family? My family is not here because my mother
wants to get rid of me and I want to stay with my Father in America," said Anastasia. "They're on the decks," Isabella answered

gazing around with astonishment. Anastasia said, "Oh, okay."
There was an uncomfortable silence.
"This place doesn't look like home. There are so many people, and
a majority of the lower class and working-class people have crusts
in their eyes, which is despicably disgusting!" Mentioned Anastasia, sealing the silence like sealing a plastic bag. Isabella didn't say
anything.
"Mmmm...Hmmmm....huhu," Isabella said, which was quite
strange. It was her 'Okay, weirdo' mumble.

CHAPTER 9

Anastasia suggested they both go up to the deck so she can greet Isabella's family. They went up on A deck, and there were so many people on the ship and the dockyard below; some people were looking out from the windows in 1st class, 2nd class and 3rd class. The vessel began to make high, loud noises, and Anastasia screamed like a lunatic.

Isabella used her hands and covered Anastasia's ears.

"Thank you; we're finally moving!" whined James to father, "You love to whine, don't you, son?" He asked, but James wasn't interested in answering.

"Too...Loud! Can't... take it...No...More!!" Anastasia continued to shout.

"It's like a big steam train coming to crash into you, and you'll die, and it will hurt so bad...!" Anastasia shouted.

"The noise will go soon..." Isabella said. "Not likely!!!" Anastasia continued to shout.

Anastasia sat on the floor and closed her eyes. She noticed that there was a crow's nest, and that got her thinking...

"Why is it called a crow's nest and there are no crows?" She saw the crow's nest empty and ran to it. Isabella noticed that Anastasia was going up the pole.

"What on Earth are you doing?!" Isabella called out, but she didn't answer. Isabella ran to her and began to climb the pole.

"I can't believe I'm doing this," Isabella thought as she climbed higher.

"Where the hell is Isabella?" James asked himself. He saw them climbing up the mast. "Mother," he asked. "Is Anastasia and Isabella allowed to climb up to the crows' nest?"

"Did you just say, Anastasia?!" Mother asked.

"And all this time, everyone said she wouldn't come! Such is life!" James said, laughing. Mother didn't say anything.

She looked at the mast and saw Isabella climbing up the pole along with Anastasia. She was about to pass out.

"What is she doing??!!" she shouted and ran to the pole. People began to realise that Isabella and Anastasia were climbing up the crow's nest. They finally got to the top and looked out.

"Why did you come up here?" asked Isabella,

"I wanted to see a crow in the nest and check if it was a lie because I don't like lies and I don't see a nest here, but I got distracted because I like the view. Why did you follow me? I wasn't going to die, but I like people coming to help me, so I won't be all sad and alone," said Anastasia.

"Because you were going, and you're not going to be safe, and you'll be all alone," Isabella answered.

Anastasia began to stand in front of the crow's nest, and Isabella freaked out.

"You're going to fall, get down from there!" but Anastasia tried hard not to listen.

"Calm down; we're not going to die, are we now?! Because if I were scared I would scream and I'll fall off the mast and cry or die because of the sudden shock; the view here is impeccable!" Anastasia shouted back.

Isabella looked out at the sea; the water did look a bit nice and calm. The water was slowly moving.

"I don't know why the water is tasty and fresh because it's cold and you can drown," said Anastasia.

Isabella then turned to the right and saw a tsunami of a crowd. Everyone was shouting and cheering as the boat moved away from the dock, little by little.

"Come on!" Anastasia shouted, "Let's say bye to everyone!" Isabella looked at the crowd.

"Maybe you're right," Isabella whispered to Anastasia, but she was too quiet under the noise of cheering and shouting. Isabella wanted to tell Anastasia that it wasn't so scary. So she moved closer to Anastasia so she could hear her.

"Why's Anastasia suddenly deaf?!" Isabella thought to herself.

CHAPTER 10

James, Mother and Father ran up to the main mast along with two crewmen.

 "Er... Can you little girls come down here?!!" shouted the man but the girls didn't hear.

"Do your job properly, and get my children off that mucky post!!" Mother shouted. The man looked at Mother as if he was about to cry.

"...Or we could just leave them there; it'll be a win-win! No one will have to disturb you!!" James smiled happily.

"If I could choose who I can stick at the top of that mast this second, sadly, it'll be you," Mother said angrily to James. Thankfully that kept James's mouth shut because he would've found himself floating on the sea, screaming for his life back, and hearing his Mother talking about where his funeral will be; but in a simpler term, he would've got thrown out of the ship by Mother into the cold water.

Isabella heard them shout at them again, so she finally sat in front of the crow's nest.

"Anastasia!! We have to get down from here!! Those crewmembers might climb up the mast and kill us!!! We might fall off!!" she shouted to Anastasia.

"Fine let's go down, and please stop shouting; you are making my ears hurt. When someone screams I need to lie on the floor, and there are no floors to lie on right now, and I like the floor because I see bugs and I like bugs when they crawl on me, so I calm down," Anastasia said climbing down the mast. Isabella quickly came down with her. The crewmembers were already coming up the pole, and they started going down.

"Well done, men.

You came too late, so get down here quickly! You should've allowed the kids to come down first!" Mother shouted at them once they hit the floor.

"And how were we meant to do that Miss clever-clogs?! Huh, we don't get all year 'round for you and your messed up mouth to answer!" the man said.

"The way you should've let them down is the same way you let them go up; if you were more practical about things, you would've seen them climbing up!!" Mother shot back.
The man was about to punch Mother hard in the face, but the first guy pulled him back.

"Let's just go, I totally hate my life right now!" the first man said.
"Me too," the other guy said, and they walked away.
"Better for you to hate your life than to like it!" James laughed at the first guy.
"Shut up, Sir!" The other crewman said. James did that unpleasant face to the man just like what he did to Isabella before in the morning. The two girls landed back on the floor; Anastasia felt a little weary; she felt like it's been years since she's been on 'solid ground.'

Mother and Father walked towards Isabella and Anastasia with James behind them.
"Look, Isabella, I know you only want to have fun, but that was extremely dangerous!!!!," Said Mother.
"Your mother is right. There was a high chance that you and Anastasia could have fallen from there!! Is there anything else that you have to say about this, James?!" Father asked, looking at James.
"What I have to say about this is... I want to go inside, and I don't care," James said.
"Don't cause any more trouble," warned Father.
" But forget problems; let's just be happy that now Anastasia's here! We all thought you wouldn't come!!" James laughed.
"Well, I did come, and now I can spend some days on the ship with you lot. I hope it'll be fun..."Anastasia said.

"In a couple of hours, we'll all go and have some tea. Remember to wear your tea dresses " Mother said to Anastasia and Isabella. The two girls nodded their heads.
"You gotta be KIDDING me? I hope you won't bring your stupid dollies and play tea party or somethin' !" James shouted.
"Sorry, James but we're 'adulting you' like what I said before!" Father happily answered. James grumbled to himself.
"Anyway, I wanted to introduce you to a pal I have just met. His name is

Edward Mantoos, and he has a lot of things in common with me!" Father said.

"Does it include constant annoyance?" James asked sarcastically.

Isabella and Mother laughed.

"That's a bit rude," Anastasia said matter-of-factly.

"Sorry, James, but he doesn't have any rudeness like you," Father spat back happily. Mother and Isabella laughed again.

"He wants to meet us in the 1st class dining saloon with his family," Father later said.

"Then we shouldn't keep him waiting shall we now?!" Mother said.

They went into the lift down to D deck to go to the dining saloon.

CHAPTER 11

"I'm not so excited to meet these strangers..." Anastasia said to Isabella as Father was 'sure' of where the dining saloon is.
"Don't worry, Anastasia; if you don't want to talk to them, don't talk to them," Isabella answered, Anastasia, nodded her head slowly.
"Don't talk at all..." She repeatedly said.

"We've been here TWICE! Do you have an idea where you're taking us about, Alfred?!" Mother asked as she looked around.
"I'm pretty sure that I do know where I'm going," Father said.
"Keep lying to yourself, as if it'll make you a better person," James mumbled, but no one heard him.

They arrived and found them sitting on a table.
"You made it, You made it! Fantastic!!" Edward said, excited to see his new friend.
"Of course I made it, the whole family came," Father said as they firmly shook hands.
"This is my wife, Helenton," Father said as he introduces Mother into the conversation.
"Nice to meet you, sir," Mother kindly said.
"I'm Bridie, Edward's wife," Bridie said as she and Mother exchanged kisses on the cheek.
"Well, that's an unfortunate name," James said to Anastasia.
Anastasia didn't reply; instead, she just stared at Bridie's hat.

"Come, come. Let's all sit down," Edward said. James had to sit next to Rosemary. Rosemary sat next to Anastasia. Anastasia sat next to Bridie who sat next to Mother who sat next to Isabella who sat next to Daphne who sat next to Father who sat next to Edward, all in a round table.

"I can't believe they're storing cars in the ship!" shouted Father
"It's genuinely exceptional!
"Titanic is the ship that's unsinkable, remember? Obviously it'll be able to carry such a load," laughed the gentleman named Edward Mantoos. He was wearing a brown striped morning suit with a gold-

en pocket watch and was wearing plain white gloves.
Everyone else didn't laugh.

His wife, Bridie Mantoos, was wearing a sophisticated white
tailored walking suit with a golden lining around the bottom of the
jacket. She wore black boots and a big emerald necklace. She was
holding a white lace parasol, on the other hand, she held a white
walking purse. Her hair was brown and was tied into a bun, her
eyes were also brown. Bridie wore a massive picture hat.

Her oldest daughter, Daphne, was wearing a lace wrap over a dress;
it had an arctic- colour rhinestone, pinned at the side of her waist
with a black and white floral kimono. Her hair was brown and curly,
tied in a bun and she had a white ribbon knotted around her bun.
Her earrings were teardrop-shaped pearls, and she had mesh wrist
gloves.

Rosemary was wearing a red silk dress with golden neck linen. She
was carrying a long piece of white fur around her with a picture
hat; ostrich feathers sprang out of her hat. Rosemary had a walking
purse, and her hair was red and in a plait as a bun; Rosemary's eyes
were blue. She wore flat white shoes, and it had a red rhinestone in
the centre of her footwear.

James noticed Edward gave him a long annoying long stare. "Why
is this IDIOT keep on looking at me?!" James whispered to Anastasia across the table. Anastasia shrugged her shoulders.
"Just ask him probably; that's what I would do..." Anastasia replied.
James didn't say anything. No one was talking; apart from Edward
and Father.

CHAPTER 12

"Oh, Edward, I see you're looking at my son a lot, this is James that I was talking to you about," Father said as he dragged James into the conversation.

"Why were 'you lot' talking about me?" James asked. No one answered that question.

"And this is our daughter, Isabella," Mother said.

"She's cuter than I presumed," Rosemary said.

"No, whatever your name is! Isabella is known across the world for causing trouble!" James said.

"My name is Rosemary," She said. Isabella glared at James.

"More like 'Rosescary'!" James laughed as he told the waiter that he would like a glass of water. Rosemary stared at James with revulsion and James gave her an unfriendly glare.

"And who are you, little girl? You haven't spoken much," Bridie asked Anastasia.

Anastasia stared at Bridie with no expression on her face.

She then mumbled to herself and put her face on the table.

"Did she hear what I just said?" Bridie asked.

"This is Anastasia; she's friends with Isabella, and she doesn't act like many children in the world. You see, she has autism, so she doesn't really speak as much like other kids," Mother said. Bridie nodded her head.

Anastasia awkwardly continued to stare at Bridie.

"James doesn't seem too nice to me," Daphne later said to Mother.

"Yeah, did you even discipline him properly?" Rosemary asked.

Mother didn't answer that question.

"I'm gonna punch each of your faces if you don't shut up!" James warned.

Rosemary, Daphne and Bridie gasped.

"I need to talk to James so we'll be back," Mother said.

"Wait, what?!" James asked.

"Get up from the chair," Mother said.

James got up from the chair and Mother whispered into his ear.

"I've taken you to etiquette lessons no longer than a month ago!
Now behave how those teachers told you to or else you'll have to be
taken to Finishing school!"
"Finishing school is for depressed people!" James said.
"So are you gonna keep yourself together?!" Mother asked.
James nodded his head, and they went back and sat on the table.
"I would love a James in my life, so confident and always talking
his mind!" Edward stated as his big hand patted James hard on the
back. James moved away from him then stared at Edward in an
annoying way.

"Why would you want James, Father? Don't you know James is so
obnoxious, vile, stupid, ugly, unpleasant, repulsive, arrogant, despi-
cable, mind-corrupted, annoying, angry, aggressive, rude, unfriendly, freakish, hateful, clumsy cold-hearted, cruel, dirty, evil, gawky,
sarcastic and bad-mouthed!" Daphne said, feeling proud of herself.
 Rosemary, Bridie, Edward, Mother and Father, Anastasia and Isabella stared at her in disapproval.

James clenched his fists together under the table and began to
breathe loud and fast. Isabella thought he'd start swearing at her.
The waiter came back with a cup of water and chocolate.
"Thanks!" James shouted and gulped the water down very quickly.
He threw the chocolate bar to Anastasia, and she smiled.
"What's this fool doing?" Bridie asked.
Daphne shrugged her shoulders.

Then he calmly told Edward, as his eye twitched with anger,
"I think, Edward, I want to be a fighter, and I need someone to train
on. Since Daphne doesn't look so needed in your family, do you
mind if I take Daphne and exercise on her? We'll give you coverage
of £100 a month, and when she finally dies, you can use that money
for her funeral, even though not many people will come. I'll get a
contract for you to sign soon, until then, is that an agreement?"
He did that same unpleasant smile to Daphne as he did to Isabella.
Everyone stared at James in disgust apart from Mother.

She was laughing as loud as she could, and her voice echoed across the table. Bridie stared at Mother in horror.

"Are you even for real?!" She asked angrily.

Mother shrugged her shoulders and continued to laugh.

"Let's pretend that this all never happened and have a little look at our guest bedrooms," Edward replied,

"Or we can continue to laugh at how ashamed, and funny Daphne looks!" Mother shouted, and everyone looked at her face; it was sweaty, bulging and her eyes were all red; as if she was put into an oven. Everyone else started to laugh.

Then Edward said to everyone, which wasn't so relevant, "I got another daughter, and her name is Alice. She's a maid on the Titanic."

"A MAID?!" Mother and Isabella blurted out inconveniently.

Edward nodded his head as an awkward silence started.

"That says a lot about your family," James mumbled looking at the ground.

"Why would you do that? Isn't it odd that Rosemary and Daphne aren't maids?" Isabella asked. Mother quickly shushed her.

"Are you her mother or something?!" Rosemary asked.

Isabella didn't answer.

"She may not be her mother, but her REAL one is doing a bad job anyway!" Mother cackled like a witch.

"She deserves it anyway!" laughed James to himself.

"I'm going to slap that smirk off you if you continue to say bad stuff about my daughters, you rascal!" Edward's wife told James.

"Smack me? You'll be dead before you raise your hand," James angrily threatened.

"Let's all calm down now," Edward said, "We may have different beliefs about each other, but we're all friends," Father agreed and nodded his head. James glared hard at Bridie. She frowned harder at him.

"Let's go back to our room, Father," James said.

CHAPTER 13

James unlocked the door.
"Your room looks a lot like mine..." Anastasia said to Isabella as they sat on the sofa.
"Maybe we should go to your bedroom sometime," Isabella replied, "The maid is here,"

"The lady doesn't seem much trouble," Father stated. James looked into the promenade deck. Alice was in there, sitting on a chair and folding clothes.
She wore a black long dress that had a white apron.
She had a roasted-pecan hair tied in a bun and her eyes were chocolate brown.

An odd feeling that James has never experienced went through his body once he saw Alice. He began to feel very sweaty and he couldn't take his eyes off her.
"Can I help you with anything, sir?" Alice asked kindly.
 James' face flushed coral red, "Uh...no," James said, scratching his head, looking at the floor. He looked at her and Alice smiled at him. James did it too.
He went into the bathroom and flushed the toilet for no particular reason.

Father removed his black jacket and put it in the closet. James did the same thing.
"Where am I going to sleep?" James asked as he looked into all the other rooms.
"You'll be sleeping on that sofa there," answered Mother as she pointed at where Anastasia and Isabella were.
There was velvet green with dirty green cushions. James despised the shade.
"ME?! SLEEP ON THAT PUKE SOFA?!" James shouted.
"Watch your language, James!" Father said from the other room.
"I don't have to watch my language! I don't want to sleep on the sofa," James shouted, "Where's Isabella going to sleep, huh?"
"She'll sleep in another room with Anastasia," Mother said.

"Oh really?!!" Isabella squealed.

"We're having a sleepover," Anastasia said.

"You gotta be kidding me!!" James muttered as he kicked the sofa when no one was looking. Isabella went into the promenade deck and saw Alice; Isabella hadn't spoken to her.

"Anastasia, I want you to get your doll so we can play tea parties in our promenade deck. Get your doll," Isabella said once Anastasia got into the promenade deck.

Anastasia said okay and banged her door open and ran to her room.

"Hello, Miss Victoria; where did you keep Blanche Dakota Consuelo; my doll?" Anastasia asked.

"I just popped her on your bed; she looked like she needed a rest," Victoria laughed, sitting in the armchair beside the sofa. Anastasia ran to her bedroom and got Blanche Dakota Consuelo.

Anastasia ran out of the room and crashed into Rosemary.

"You have to watch where you're going, Anastasia!" Rosemary shouted.

Anastasia stared at her, then ran away into the Norflook's hotel place or something. Alice was reading a book on the sofa. James was...somewhere.

"I'm back!" Anastasia said as she ran to a deck chair with her doll, Blanche.

"Fantastic, I got my tea-party set too," Isabella smiled as she ordered the cutlery, teacups and the teapot on top of a white cotton blanket.

"Hello, my name is Lotta Spring!" Isabella imitated as she shook Lotta Spring around, "What's your name?" 'Lotta Spring' asked Anastasia's doll. "Her name is Blanche Dakota Consuelo, and she can't speak so I'll speak for her," Anastasia said.

"Blaunk what Conleo?!" Isabella asked as she looked at Blanche Dakota Consuelo.

"Blan-che," Anastasia said

"Blan-che," Isabella answered.

"Da-ko-ta," Anastasia said next.

"Da-ko-ta," Isabella replied

"Con-suelo," Anastasia said.

"Con-suelo," Isabella repeated too.

"Blanche Dakota Consuelo," Anastasia said.
"Blanche Dakota Consuelo," repeated Isabella.
"I've never heard that name before, Anastasia. Is it foreign?" Isabella asked. Anastasia answered, yes.
"Blanche is a French name, Dakota is a Native American name-" Anastasia said but got interrupted.
"I've never heard of a country called Native American?!" Isabella said.

"You're right; Native America is not a country because they were a civilisation of people in the olden times; like Greeks, Romans. They lived in tribes all over America and were apparently 'discovered' by Christopher Columbus." Anastasia said.
"He called them Indians because he thought that they landed in the Indies; which is very silly of him; didn't he have a map or something?" Anastasia asked. Isabella laughed.

"And Consuelo is a Spanish name so yeah, Blanche Dakota Consuelo is my doll's name," Anastasia said.
"Do you want real food for our tea party?!" Isabella asked happily. Anastassia nodded her head.
"I shall get Alice to get us some biscuits, cookies, fruit and tea!" Isabella said as she stood up with Lotta Spring.
"I love, love cookies and fruits; make sure they get us grapes though," Anastasia reminded.
"I'll try," Isabella laughed happily and opened the french doors, but someone appeared.

CHAPTER 14

"Bonjour petite girls! Comment se passe ta journée?" James happily asked as he barged his way through Isabella to sit on a deck chair.
"No need for such horrible French!!" Isabella said and was about to walk away.
"I've been hearing what you lot were talking about; tea parties, Native Americans and then my favourite part - food! Do you mind if you add chocolate to the shopping list, and some juice?" James asked.

"Aren't you the kind of person who drinks wine from a bucket of ice?" Isabella asked. James quickly shook his head.
"Wine tastes far too bitter, and people like that are in a snob group!" James answered.
"Maybe you should start drinking wine, you are a snob!" Isabella laughed.
"If you don't shut up, I'll slap you so hard, that even the devil will have pity for you!" James warned. Isabella glared at him.
"You're not eating our treats!" Isabella said as she folded her arms across her chest, looking away from James.
"Yeah, you mean person!! You don't deserve it at all!" Anastasia said glaring at James.

"WHAT?! Come on, Isabella, you're better than this!! Come on I'll do anything, pleeeeeeeeeeaaaaaaaaaaaaaaaaaaaaasssssssssssssssssssss ssssssssssssssssssssssssssssssssssssssssssssssssss?!" James begged as he kneeled in front of Isabella. She looked at him as if she had sympathy but she was actually being sarcastic.
"Lots of S's," Anastasia said as she lay on the floor.
"Did you say anything...?" Isabella asked. James didn't say anything because he knew that he'll have to do something that he despises.
"Yes, I said, anything. So what do you want me to do?" James sluggishly replied. Isabella thought for a long time.
"What should he do?" Isabella asked.
"Mmmmm...Maybe he can get a toy and play with us!!" Anastasia suggested as James wished his life was over.

"Fantastic idea!" Isabella said, "I'll get a toy for you, James."
"Help me!!!!" James wailed impolitely.

Isabella walked out of the promenade deck and went to Alice.
She realised that both Mother and Father weren't in.
"Alice, where are my parents?" Isabella asked.
"I don't know, Isabella," Alice replied.
"Well, I actually came here for something else. You see, Anastasia, James and I want to have a tea party with our toys, and we want real food. So do you mind bringing us biscuits, cookies, fruit and tea and chocolates?" Isabella asked.
"Yes but hang on, James is actually playing tea parties with the two of you. The blonde tall one?" Alice asked, rather surprised.
 "He's only playing with us because he loves chocolate," Isabella answered.
"I'll be on my way, then," Alice answered and left the room.
Isabella came back into the bedroom and got her teddy bear. It was Isabella's 6th birthday present from James. She didn't really like it, and she hadn't even thought of a name for it, so she had to think of one,
"Candy? Fluffy? Let me just call it Poopster! It is a waste of my life," Isabella thought, and she ran to the promenade deck where Anastasia and James were.

"Looks like you've got the 6th birthday present that I gave you huh? I didn't think of its gender so you can decide," James cackled.
"I don't like it so I'll give it both genders," Isabella answered.
"That's scientifically impossible!" Anastasia said.
"Well, not anymore, it's not! Things have got a whole lot funnier!" James laughed after his long cackle.
"What's its name?" Anastasia asked as she stroked Blanche Dacota Consuelo's hair.
"It's called Poopster," answered Isabella, feeling sorry for Poopster's name.
"What kind of name is Poopster?! It's deferentially not a different name!" Anastasia blurted out.
"Hey, everyone, things are different, you know!" Isabella said.
"This funny thing has gone to a whole new level!" James laughed.

"Well that's fantastic, you can take Poopster, and you'll play with him!" Isabella smiled. She threw the teddy into James's laps and sat on a deck chair, waiting for Alice to come.

"Let's start playing," suggested Anastasia.
"No way! I'm only playing when the food is here!" James shouted.
"Play now, you get the food. Don't play now, you don't get anything, and you'll cry as we eat our food, and we'll eat it slowly." Isabella threatened happily. James didn't say anything for a few seconds.
"Let's play then," he later mumbled.

"Good to hear!" Anastasia said as she pushed James off the chair and onto the floor with a big THUD!
"Ouch Anastasia! Watch yourself!" James yelled.
"Stop shouting too much! You know it makes my ears hurt!" Anastasia hissed as she lied on the blanket.
James used his back and slid to the blanket, tossing Poopster around.
Isabella sat at the rim with Lotta Spring.

"Okay, so what are we gonna do?!" 'Poopster' asked.
"What we're gonna do is play hide and seek!" 'Lotta Spring' replied.
"Blanche Dakota Consuelo wants to count," Anastasia said. "1, 2, 3..." Anastasia said, starting to count, James ran out of the room and flung Poopster into the toilet.
"That's where you fit in, Poop-Star!!" James smirked while he hid inside a closet. Isabella ran into Mother's room and hid under the bed with Lotta Spring.

"No one will find us Lotta Spring; these tassels make us invisible!" Isabella said happily. Lotta Spring didn't reply as usual.
"20! Ready or not, here I come!!!!" Anastasia screamed, got Blanche Dakota Consuelo and ran into the toilet.
"Stop the game!! Everyone come." Anastasia said, looking at poor Poopster.
James and Isabella walked out of their hiding places.
"James, where is Poopster?" Isabella asked.

"Somewhere where he belongs," James happily answered. Isabella looked at him suspiciously. Then she did her 'Okay, weirdo' mumble.

James and Isabella walked to the bathroom to see what Anastasia was rambling about.
"James, why is Poopster in the toilet?!" Anastasia asked, putting her hands on her hips.
"Because that's where he belongs!" James cheerfully answered.
"What do you mean; 'Where he belongs'?" Isabella asked, slightly confused.
"Don't you get it: Poop-star! Where do you think poop belongs?" James asked. Anastasia started to moan, just thinking of poop.
"Poop belongs in the toilet," Isabella answered.
"Exactly! And he's a star at being in the toilet; Poop- star! I would've flushed him down the toilet, you know, but I felt 'sorry' for the guy, so you know, I left him there; like floating poop!" James answered.
"That's so disgusting! I'm out of here!!" Anastasia cried, and she ran into the promenade deck.
"Get Poopster out of the toilet," Isabella requested. James looked at her as if he was going to puke. Isabella rolled her eyes, then responded furiously. "You heard what I said, get Poopster out of the toilet! Poopster is MY teddy, and you threw it in the bathroom so get Poopster out, wash him, then we'll continue to play,"
"You're so mean!" James said like a baby as he got Poopster out of the toilet throwing it on the sofa.

Alice opened the door with a tray of grapes, biscuits, chocolates and tea.
"I'm back, Isabella!" She said. James began to blush again at the sight of her.
 "What's wrong with you?" Isabella asked.
"Shut up!!" James screamed, turning redder. Isabella looked harder at James, "You not telling me something. Why do you flush every time Alice is around?"
"You shut the damn up or else!" James shouted even louder.
"Fine," Isabella said, and she walked to Alice and got the tray off her.
"Thank you, Alice," Isabella smiled.

"You're welcome," Alice replied. She then saw the wet teddy on the sofa, "Um, who was silly enough to put a wet teddy on the sofa?" She requested.

Isabella looked at James, "Looks like that person can answer for himself,"

James scratched his head, turning red and didn't reply. He went to close the door.

"Alice, you can eat with us too," James smiled, his face turning to the colour of crimson. Isabella looked at him.

"That sounds nice. I'm famished; thanks, James," Alice says, happily.

James's stomach almost exploded with happiness and joy.

"Hmm," Isabella said.

"What?!" James shouted as Alice left.

"Sweaty palms..." Isabella said, touching James's hand.

"Don't you touch me," James snapped.

"Always blushing," Isabella said, "What's going on with you?"

"I swear I'll murder you if you don't bug off!" James yelled.

"Don't kill me..." Isabella whispered with fear in her eyes. James sighed then said, "You do realise that I'm a Christian so I can't kill you," he walked into the promenade deck and sat on the floor next to Alice. Isabella quickly followed.

"Are we finished talking about poop?" She asked.

"Quite indeed," Alice answered, being thankful that she wasn't here the whole time.

CHAPTER 15

"When are your mother and father coming?" Alice asked.

Isabella shrugged her shoulders. The food was nowhere near finished, and Isabella was already full.

"We spoke to your family, Alice, and they're very bothersome and annoying," Isabella said while she took a large bite at his cookie.

"I don't really understand why they're a bit...weird," Alice sighed. "But your parents seem friendly,"

"Like you," James blurted out without knowing. Alice stared at him.

"Holy cow..." James whispered, turning redder than ever, putting his hands over his face.

Isabella's mouth dropped open, "You've said nothing nice in your life, James!!! Alice, what's in this food?! It's poisoning James!!!"

"It's not poisoning!" Anastasia said, "James is simply saying something kind,"

"Well, thanks for the compliment, if you're not usually good," Alice said reddening. She gave him an affiliative smile. James said nothing, even though his thoughts were all pink and yellow. No one spoke for a while after that.

"I've learnt that Alice has two sisters; the oldest is Daphne and the second oldest is Rosemary," Anastasia said. Alice laughed.

"I hate the word second!" James said.

"Why?" Anastasia asked as she sipped some tea.

"Because if you come in second place, you don't know if you are first or last and no one cares for seconds. Also, if you are a second child, you don't know if you are essential. For instance, the oldest need their parents to help them with the important stuff, like going to university or something like that. And if you are the youngest child, you need your parents to help you with everything, because you're stupid and you can't do anything for yourself! A second child is just there doing nothing; have nothing to do," James responded. No one said anything for a while.

"And what if you are a second child and the youngest, because I'm both?" Isabella asked. James laughed.

"That's both worse for you; you are both stupid and have nothing to do!!" He answered.

"That's a pity," Alice mumbled.

"But being the oldest is the best! You get to decide what you want, and you get it first. Not to mention that the youngest always gets the scraps for everything." James said.
"But, if you are a second child, you don't need to be the dumb one like the youngest, or the reliable one like the oldest," Isabella said.
"I think being the youngest is the best," Anastasia said.
"Because when you are the youngest, your parents are more likely to be with you, showing that you can't do anything by yourself. And if the world was like you only die by age, the oldest will die first, and you'll be the last to die," Anastasia said, taking all the grapes.

"But what if you got an idiotic father who loves the oldest child more than the younger child, and a stupid mother who likes their younger child more than the older child?" James asked.
Anastasia didn't answer.
"Let's continue to eat; the tea is getting cold," Alice replied. Everyone agreed to that.

"Alice," James said blushing.
"What is it?" She asked.
"We haven't all got to know about you," James said, looking at the ground.
"So?" She asked.
"We've told you about us, so let's know more about you," Anastasia answered cheerfully.
"What do you want to know about me?"Alice asked.
"Your age, height, private life, what you think about anything, your family," Anastasia said.
"I don't know your ages," Alice said.
"I'm nine, Isabella's nine, James's fifteen," Anastasia replied.
"Well, I'm nineteen," Alice said.
 Mother unlocked the door and screamed, "We're back!!!"
"I can't believe they are here so soon!!" James whined inconveniently.
"I like your parents," Anastasia said as she ate the last grape.
"Easy for you to say, you don't even know how annoying they can

be!" James moaned.

Father walked to the promenade deck and saw James, Isabella, Anastasia and Alice all eating together.
"Wow, looks like the four of you are bonding!" Father cheered.
"I only bond with people when there's food involved," James answered.
"James only bonded with Alice. He called her friendly," Isabella said.
"SHUT UP!!!!!!!!" James screamed. Anastasia giggled to herself.
Father looked at him, funnily, "Have you found love, my boy?"
Alice and James looked at each other then blushed. James glared at the three of them.
Isabella, Anastasia and Father screamed with laughter. Alice said nothing.
"CAN YOU STOP?!" James snapped.
"James and Alice sitting in a tree, K-I-S-S-I-N-G!!" Father and Isabella laughed.
James raged with anger and aggressively stormed into the bathroom and slammed the door shut. Alice left after him.
"What happened with James?" Mother asked.
"I pulled off his funny bone," Father laughed.
"More like his love bone!" Isabella corrected.
Father and Isabella chuckled.
Mother shook her head, "You know James ain't a happy person when you laugh at him,"
"At the end of the day, it ain't me getting my face all ugly," Father laughed.
"What shall we do now?" Anastasia asked Mother.
"Well, you've finished eating, you lot can have a nap," Mother answered.
"A NAP?!" Anastasia and Isabella yelled.
"I'm not -1 year old!" Isabella groaned. "What are you, Mother, a governess? You don't need to tell a 9-year-old girl to have a nap. I'm not on the potty training stage!"
"Well, that's too bad!" Mother said.
Anastasia and Isabella angrily got out some duvet, lay it on the floor and went to the dressing room to change into their nighties.

CHAPTER 16

Anastasia and Isabella suggested they sleep on the promenade deck so they can close the doors and not rest.
"James is still in there," Anastasia said.
"He really got angry. I hope he's okay," Isabella replied under the covers. "I doubt that," Anastasia whispered.
"He's always angry, but never like this," Isabella said worriedly.
"Don't fear, the problem will be solved. Let's just get some rest," Anastasia smiled. Isabella smiled weakly. Isabella and Anastasia closed their eyes and went to sleep.

"James, can you hear me?! Get out of the toilet and speak to me!" Father said, banging on the door.
"He's still not answering?" Mother asked. Father nodded.
"Do you need anything I can help you with, Mam?" Alice asked.
"Do you know how to get a man out of the bathroom?" Mother asked. Alice shook her head.
"Then you can do whatever you want," Mother smiled. Alice went and got out a book and began to read on the sofa.
"Let me try something," Mother said. She walked over to the bathroom door and told James, "If you come out, James I'll give you another violin,"
James didn't reply.
"I hope he's okay," Father whispered as he sat back.

 2 hours passed, and Mother looked at the clock, and it was 3.05 pm.
"Time to wake the children up," Father said as he closed the book he was reading. James was still in the toilet.
"I call dibs not to wake 'em!" Father shouted as he touched his nose-first.
Mother rolled her eyes and groaned, "It's going to be your turn next,"
But Father laughed to himself.
Mother tiptoed into the deck room and saw them all sleeping,

"What stupid children! Thinking that they don't need a nap!" Mother whispered happily.

She got hold of all their duvets and pulled it off them.

"AAAHHHH!" The girls shouted.

"What was that for?!" Isabella shrieked.

"Okay, ladies, get up! Isabella, you need to wear your tea dress!" Mother smiled.

"Anastasia, I don't suppose you have a tea dress too?" Mother asked Anastasia.

"I have a tea dress, Mrs Norflook; I shall change in my room then," Anastasia said, and she ran out of their parlour suite, into her room. Anastasia found Victoria reading a book in the parlour.

"Hello Anastasia, what are you doing in your room?" Victoria asked as she went inside.

"I cannot find my tea dress!!" Anastasia cried as she threw her clothes out of the hanger.

"It's right here, Alice told me you will soon go for a tea party with the Norfolks, so I put all the things you need to wear on your bed," Victoria answered.

Anastasia saw her lace dress, lace gloves, flat ivory shoes, a white hat with a feather and her white tights on her bed. Anastasia wished she hadn't messed up her room because now she felt sick with all the mess which made her head not right; Anastasia's face turned red as she rocked back and forth on her bed. She then ran to the toilet and began to vomit.

Victoria ran behind her and heard Anastasia vomiting in the toilet. Victoria rubbed Anastasia's back as she stopped vomiting. She quickly ran to the sink and used the tap to rinse her mouth and face because she didn't want to see her puke or else she'll barf again.

"Flush the toilet..." Anastasia said to Victoria, who, when she saw the vomit in the toilet, she made that puking noise and quickly flushed the toilet.

"I need to leave; I don't fancy this stinking fume..." Anastasia sighed as she went into the other room. Victoria carried her clothes to her room.

"I'll be in the parlour reading, if you need me, just say my name," said Victoria.

Anastasia stared at Victoria as she left. She closed her eyes and lay on the floor thinking about the tea party. She then began to dress up.

CHAPTER 17

Five minutes later, Victoria heard Anastasia screaming.
"I said to call my name not scream like an insane girl," Victoria said as she ran into the room. She found Anastasia screaming as she tried to pull up her tights.
"What's the matter?!" Victoria asked.
"My tights won't go up!! And my hands are hurting!!" Anastasia screamed as she began to pull her hair. Victoria looked at what she was moaning about. She was standing on the rest of the tights so she couldn't pull them up. Victoria rolled her eyes.

"Stand up, Anastasia," Victoria sighed. Anastasia stood up from the bed. She pulled up Anastasia's tights for her.
"I can't understand that you require my assistance to pull up your tights; you are nine Anastasia," Victoria said.

"My hands hurt..." Anastasia whispered. Victoria then told her to sit on the chair so she could put on her shoes. Anastasia put on her gloves and took her pocket watch which her father gave her. Victoria took Anastasia to the dresser so she could brush her hair. Once she was done, she told Anastasia that she'll put her gold earrings on, but Anastasia screamed, "What's the problem now?!" Victoria asked.

"What if you stab me? I haven't known you for a long time. But if you try, I'll use my comb and poke your eye," Anastasia warned as she looked at Victoria from the mirror putting her pocket watch on her head then putting on her hat. Victoria put on her earrings and told Anastasia to knock on Mr and Mrs Noflook's door and wait for an answer.

"Why?" Anastasia asked.
"Because the males might still be changing; and it's polite," Victoria said.
She adjusted Anastasia's hat on Anastasia and said bye. Anastasia did not say anything.

CHAPTER 18

"James, please come out!! What are you doing?" Isabella begged, banging on the door.

"Why?!!" James shouted back. It was a little shocking to hear his voice, but Isabella replied, "You're scaring me, just get out already!!"

There was a little silence, but then the door unlocked and James came out. His eyes were all red like he's been crying.

"Have you been crying?" Isabella asked.

James gave her a death stare. It was so scary with his forest-green eyes that Isabella almost cried. She stepped back, and James walked past her. James had only done it once when a man punched him in the face three years ago because James called him fat. He gave the man the death stare.

"Where have you been in the toilet, James? Do you even know that we need to meet Edward-" Father said. James gave him the death stare and a chill went down Father's spine. "Good God," Father whispered, fear in his eyes. "Just wear a suit..."

James sighed and changed into his suit.

Isabella and Father stared at each other. "How does he do it?" Isabella asked. Father shook his head, "I don't know."

Minutes went by, and James was done dressing.

"We'll be on our way," Father said, and he opened the door. Anastasia was standing in front of them, and James asked, "Have you been standing there for some time?"

Anastasia nodded her head.

"Why?" James asked. Anastasia was about to say something, but Father told James to stop asking questions and start going to the smoking lobby and that he doesn't want to keep Edward waiting. So Father told Anastasia to get inside their room so that Mother could know that she was here.

Anastasia told Mother that she was ready to go and Mother smiled, "Fantastic! Let's start going," Mother said. Isabella was still healing from the death stare, and she limped to Anastasia.

"Are you okay?" Anastasia asked. Isabella nodded.

Mother pushed Anastasia and Isabella out of the room and locked the door.

"A- deck, here we come!!" Mother grinned.

Anastasia and Isabella walked behind Mother.

"Are you eager to see Daphne, Rosemary and Mrs Mantoos again?" Isabella asked. Anastasia shook her head.

"I don't like how she asked about me, it was not her business, and she doesn't know me and I don't know her! And there might be too many people, so I might just sit down and not look at anyone," Anastasia answered.

"I wonder if we're late..." Mother whispered to herself.

Anastasia got a golden pocket watch under her hat.

"It's 3:15 pm and 1, 2, 3, 4, etc. seconds," Anastasia answered as she put her pocket watch back under her hat.

"You keep a pocket watch on your head?!" Isabella asked, gob-smacked.

"I need to know the time at all times or else I wouldn't know what to do, when to do it and how long I should do it," Anastasia answered as she barged past someone in 1st class.

"Out of all the places, you choose to keep your pocket watch on your head?" Isabella asked. Anastasia nodded.

"It is very accessible because if I put it in my pocket, it'll be harder for me to get, for example, I got my pen, my kuna, and the little golden bear that I look at," Anastasia answered.

"Let's stop talking and start walking..." Mother said quickly.

They got to the 1st class lounge and saw Rosemary, Daphne and Bridie looking for where to sit. Than Rosemary whispered to Bridie, "Mrs Norflook and her children are here,"

"Complete rubbish!" Bridie whispered back as she walked to Mother.

"Hello, Ida," she looked at Isabella, "Nice to see your daughter, she's actually able to wear something, upper class..." Bridie said.

"I could say the same to you," Mother said as she scanned Bridie, "Only, it'll be much worse..."

Bridie didn't say anything.

"Let's sit here, near the door so you could leave anytime," Rosemary suggested.

"Amusing, second child," Mother laughed as she sat down next to Isabella and Anastasia. Then a servant walked Anastasia; she began to feel strange, and her chest began to hurt.

"Do you need anything to eat?" the man asked.

"Go away, I don't know you..." Anastasia mumbled as she turned away.

"She'll be having grapes and water," Mother said.

"All of us would like some tea and biscuits," Bridie said. The man said okay, and left.

CHAPTER 19

"I plan that once I go to America, I'll open a tailoring store in addition to a boutique," Edward said as he puffed out a vast amount of smoke into James's face. James coughed and coughed as if there was a bug in his throat.

"I say, Is everything okay, James?" Edward asked. He touched James's right shoulder. James grabbed Edward's hand, and said, "Don't you dare touch me!" He gave Edward his death stare. James let go of him, and Edward felt like he was dying.

"I don't know how he does it," Father told Edward. There was an awkward silence before Edward puffed smoke at James's face yet again. "Do you mind?!" James asked. Edward said nothing.

"James, do you want to be somewhere else?" Father asked. James just glared at Edward and walked away.

"Sorry about James's behaviour, he's been acting strange today," Father said in his 'concerned' voice.

"It's okay, Alfred. He's still my favourite," Edward laughed. Father laughed too.

"What does it feel like to have three daughters?" Father asked.

"Hmm. It can be difficult at times. All I wanted was a boy and a girl. They all want everything, especially Rosemary and Daphne. But Alice, my little girl, is a born angel. Always does the right thing, always listens and has a good sense of humour. She's nothing like her older siblings," Edward said. "What about your children?" Edward asked as he puffed out more smoke.

"Well, actually it's a disaster! They just always fight for everything. What side of the table they sit. Where they put their things. Even just the 'best' apple! According to them, the best apple is red, it has to be cold and crunchy!! I expected James to be a little bit more mature since he's twenty, but he went the opposite," Father shook his head ashamed, "At least he has musical fingers."

"Now does he? What instruments?" Edward questioned.

"Violin, harp, flute, cello, double bass, french horn and piano. Oh, he loves the piano. I have no idea how he learnt it. He bought an instrument and began to play beautiful notes," Father replied.

"Well isn't that wonderful," Edward said.

CHAPTER 20

The man came back with a big silver tray of tea, grapes and cookies. "Here you go," The man said as he put the tray in the middle of the table. Rosemary, Daphne, Bridie, Mother and Isabella said thank you. The man walked away, and Bridie said, "Here you go Rosemary and Daphne," she poured some tea into their teacups and gave them four cookies on their plate. Mother gave Anastasia her bowl of grapes and the glassful of water.
Then Mother gave Isabella her tea and cookies.
"Thanks, Mother!" Isabella smiled as she slouched on the chair and ate her cookie, making crumbles on her dress.
Mother looked angrily at Isabella, then whispered kindly in her ear, "Sit up Isabella and put your napkin on your lap; Anastasia is showing you a good example now do the same thing," Mother used her hand and pushed Isabella's back up. Isabella looked at Anastasia; she had her napkin and was eating her grapes very slowly. Isabella got her towel and placed it on her lap and sipped her tea.

"So, how's Isabella at school? Where do you plan on taking her to, for her new school?" Bridie asked.
"Isabella was one of the smartest in her class and practiced her homework 24\7. I plan on taking her to a really respected private school that has horses to ride, ballet lessons and art," Mother said.
"Is she good at ballet?" Rosemary asked. Mother nodded her head.
"She's done Swan Lake at her school and was the centre of attention," Mother said, feeling proud of Isabella.
"What have you achieved, Anastasia?" Daphne asked as she ate her last cookie.
Anastasia didn't answer.
"Come on, Anastasia, don't be shy," Isabella whispered to Anastasia.
"Fine…" She muttered to herself as she looked down at the table.
"I was able to learn how to ride a horse at the age of 6," she whispered.
"Excuse me, but what did she just say?" Rosemary asked, looking at Mother.
"She said that she learnt how to ride a horse at the age of 6," Mother

answer

"And what was the horse's name?" Daphne asked.

"Her name is Lucinda, and I don't like the name, and I won't tell you why and I'm going to stop talking to you," Anastasia answered as she looked down again.

"She is shy," Bridie said.

"Or she just hates you in general; I wouldn't be surprised!" Mother said.

Bridie, Rosemary and Daphne laughed like the kind of person who would drink tea with their pinky sticking up.

"Very funny…" Rosemary said.

"I know, honey!" Mother smiled.

James came in the room out of nowhere, sat on a table and looked around. Isabella and Mother looked at him and pretended they didn't see him.

A man walked to James and asked him, "Would you like something to eat?"

James nodded his head, "Get me water; I've had enough contaminating stuff for one day…" He muttered as he thought of some freak smoking in his face. The man gave James a 'concerned' look, then walked away.

James saw Bridie and then saw Mother and Anastasia. He ran to the dude and told him he'll be sitting next to the girl who was Anastasia.

"Let's hope her breath isn't contaminating…" the man laughed.

James gave him an unpleasant look.

"Was that meant to be funny?" James asked. The man nodded his head.

James began to laugh awkwardly. The man did the same thing. They continued to laugh and began to walk away slowly. James ran to Anastasia and startled her.

"Hello, gang!" James smiled panting. The girls stared at him.

"I just wanted to be part of the sassy talk, you know. Be part of the girly group," James said, throwing hand gestures at them. But they still didn't answer. James got a chair and sat next to Anastasia.

"Whatever, let's just pretend that a certain someone is NOT here and let's continue to talk!" Rosemary answered, rudely.

"Or, we can pretend that the certain someone IS here and we can continue to talk!" James said, doing the unpleasant smile again as usual. The girls didn't dare say anything.

The man came back with a glass of water.

"Cheers, mate!!!" James smiled. The man looked at James then walked off.

"This will be awkward..." Isabella said.

CHAPTER 21

"What are you doing here? What is this?" Rosemary asked as she made hand gestures at James rudely. James didn't answer that question.

"I don't know why you care, honey." Mother smiled. Rosemary scanned at Mother.

"May I be excused?" Rosemary asked. Mother nodded her head quickly.

"Leave, go, bye," Mother said as she waved at Rosemary.

Rosemary got her parasol and walked away quickly.

"Fantastic! Rosescary is gone, now we can talk; I hate second children a lot. So when Rosemary's gone, I'm a little more confident of my surroundings!" James said.

"That isn't true," Anastasia said as she rubbed her napkin on her mouth.

"Whatever, I'm done eating my food! Bye!" Daphne said as she walked out of the dining saloon.

Bridie sighed and said, "I better be off,"

She walked away, and Mother smiled.

"Are we going to leave as well?" Anastasia asked as she ordered the plates, cups and cutlery. Mother nodded her head.

"Can I hold your parasol, please?" Isabella begged.

"Who would want to hold a parasol, only weak people enjoy that…" James rudely blurted out.

Mother didn't answer James's comment.

"Yes, you can hold my parasol," Mother said, and they walked away.

Hours passed by, and the sky began to turn orange.

"Oh goody, we can soon go to bed!" James smiled as he looked into the window.

"Not exactly, son," Father said as he got his toothbrush and toothpaste and started to brush his teeth. James walked into the bathroom and got his toothbrush.

"What do you mean, not exactly?" James asked as he began to

brush his teeth.

"I mean we're going to have our dinner in the dining room!!!" Father replied happily. James spat out the toothpaste from his mouth.

"Eek! We're going to wear fancy clothes!!!" Isabella squealed.

"Quite obviously," Anastasia annoyingly said.

"Aaaah, Father! Now since I've brushed my teeth, when I eat my food, it'll taste disgusting!!!" James moaned.

"Good for you, James. I don't care what you hate, just change into your tuxedo so I can gel your hair," Father said a bit worried as he glanced at the gel bottle. James looked horrified.

"There is NO WAY that anyone is touching my hair!!" James shouted as he ran under the bed.

"Quit behaving like a silly cat, James!" Isabella laughed as she and Anastasia removed the duvet from James. He began to scream as if he had a heart attack. Father pulled James by the arms, off the bed and used a rope to tie him from a chair. James began to move back and forth as Father put some gel on his hair.

"Where did you get the rope from?" Alice asked as she looked for a dress for Isabella from the wardrobe.

"Found it under the sink," Father said as he began to smoothen James's hair. Alice gave him the 'concerned' look.

"I know, pretty weird, huh!" Father laughed. Alice nodded her head and turned to the wardrobe, still doing the 'concerned' look.

"Have you got a dress for me now?!" Isabella quickly asked as she jumped up and down.

Alice nodded her head.

She pulled out a blue and white gown that matches with her large blue bow. It had many floral silver patterns near the waist part of her dress, and Alice suggested she wears her white gloves and her blue necklace and earrings.

"Okie, dokie!" Isabella said as she slipped into the bathroom and slammed the door.

Anastasia asked Father if she should go and dress and Father said, "Quite indeed!"

Anastasia stared at James, and he looked like he had died, which was a shame anyway because Isabella might cry. His eyes were closed and he was looking unconscious.

CHAPTER 22

Anastasia waited for Victoria to brush her hair.

"I don't see why your hair needs brushing…" Victoria said. "It's all straight as a ruler,"
"What's that meant to mean?" Anastasia asked. Victoria didn't answer.

Anastasia wore her sailor suit, which Victoria found strange and wore her navy earrings and pendants.
"Have fun, Anastasia," Victoria whispered as she stroked the side of her hair.
"You too," Anastasia answered. She said it because it was polite.
Isabella opened Anastasia's door and told her they have to start going.
James was in the corner of the room, crying that Father put gel on his hair.
Mother was talking next to him and gave him a handkerchief.
Mother wore a lace wrap over dress with flowers near the waist of her skirt. She wore pearl earrings and a diamond necklace. She wore some kind of silver thing around her head as her hair was piled one on top of the other.

"I can't believe your brother is crying about GEL?!" Father said, laughing as he awkwardly scratched his head next to Isabella. Isabella laughed.
"James is such a baby!" Isabella muttered.
"I'll actually KILL YOU!" James shouted, "You don't know what it feels like to have toxic things on your hair!" He then gave her his death stare. His green eyes got brighter and his pupils got smaller and Isabella got so scared and she screamed, "MAKE IT STOP, PLEASE!!"
She ran behind Mother and she said, "How does he do it, Mother?"
"James, stop being so scary!" Mother demanded.
"I can do whatever I want!" James said as he ran back into the room and got some book that he was reading for two months
"Good, we're all ready! James, you'll be keeping an eye on these

little lasses," said Mother as she looked at Anastasia and Isabella.
 "Uhhhh!!!!!! Do I HAVE to, Mother?!" James whimpered.
"Yes, James, yes; or else…" Mother warned.
 "But remember kids, have fun!" Father said, showing happy movements which no one understood.

CHAPTER 23

The Titanic had stopped at Cherbourg, France. The ship was expecting more passengers tomorrow, but for now, passengers from France were coming into the Titanic.

"I can't believe more people are coming. This makes more crowd, doesn't it? But to be honest, I don't like a lot of passengers or strangers." Anastasia said to Isabella, who was adjusting her big, blue bow.

"This is going to be fun," Father said as he rubbed his hands together.
James removed his gloves and told Mother to hold it; he said it made his hands feel strange.

They all waited on the top of the grand stairs so Edward's family would come.
"Guess who's back!!" Edward shouted from the top of the step with his family. They came downstairs, and James felt like fainting.

"Mr and Mrs Norflook!" Edward proclaimed as they shook hands.
"You lot?! Pleasant to see you again!" Father said, forgetting what Edward's surname was.
"You guys better keep your mouth shut or I'll punch you into 3rd class!" James whispered to Daphne and Rosemary. The two girls exchanged their 'I don't care' looks and rolled their eyes.
"We'll talk for days!" Daphne whispered back.
"You know, if you do ANYTHING bad to my daughters, you'll be severely punished," Bridie warned.
"I don't think threatening me will sort the problem!" James warned back. "Don't..." Isabella said
"And what will you do about it, idiot?" Bridie asked.
"This," James said. He threw his book at her face, and she screamed, "OWWW!!"
"Oh my..." Anastasia re-embarked.
"That's gotta hurt..." Edward said to Anastasia, she nodded her head.

"Mother, are you okay?" Daphne and Rosemary asked.
"I don't think so!!!" Bridie shouted.
"Hopefully, that'll keep her mouth shut!" James said.

Thankfully, that kept her mouth shut for some time. Father and Mother were very embarrassed and said that James won't get any chocolate for a whole year. James didn't really care, as long as Bride was dead, 'order will be restored in the galaxy'.

They finally got to the dining room, and Isabella was quite confused.
"I thought this place would be a ball…" Isabella muttered.
"What? You think Cinderella will appear with her' charming prince', well sister, this ain't the late 17s" James blurted. Isabella glared at James. "I'm not as dumb as you think!!" She quietly hissed, but James wasn't listening.

They all somehow walked to a nine-seater table and went to sit down. Anastasia continued to stare at Bridie, but she didn't notice- which was good. It was quite awkward for a start because everyone had nothing to say.
James threw his book on the table; it spooked everyone for a little bit.
"Well, that was a waste of my life!" James grouched as he slumped grimly on his chair.
"What do you mean, 'waste of your life', son?" inquired Edward. James groaned to himself before explaining. "I was reading some book about a detective who was finding the dead horse in the back of a neglectful bin. The man spent two years to find the murderers, but then he didn't. Super stupid of the person. And I spent about two months finding the murderer who killed the donkey. And I'm NOT your son!!"
"Well sorry that you didn't find the murderers; she possibly wishes that she didn't slay a frail donkey," Father said.
"Not a chance…" James mumbled.

CHAPTER 24

Ten minutes and 38 seconds of total silence; very awkward if you ask me… No one said a word for 10.34 minutes. How sad...

CHAPTER 25

A servant came to ask them what they wanted to eat. They told him, and he said that their meals would come in about 5 to 10 minutes. Mother said thank you, and the man roamed away like a weirdo.

"What should we talk about-" Edward said, but he got interrupted by Anastasia.
"Look, that's John Jacob Astor IV… he's a multi-millionaire."
"WHERE? WHERE?!" James quickly asked as he scanned the room like a meerkat in the grasslands.
"Just there," Anastasia whispered.
He was walking around shaking many hands of others with his beautiful wife, Madeleine Astor.

"EEK! I adore Mr Astor IV!!! He sounds so...cool!" James smiled as he stared at him like a TV.
"Why don't you say hello to him?" Isabella asked.
"Are you sick in the head? Oh yes, you are sick in the head, and I don't blame you!" James hissed.
"This may be the last time we see him, James and he looks so 'cool'," Isabella said. James didn't respond. He asked if he and Isabella could be excused and Rosemary told him to go away.
They walked behind the Astors for a little bit, and Isabella got sick and tired of how scared James was.
"Just say, HELLO!" Isabella whined, and she pushed James at John Jacob Astor.
"I'm gonna kill you for real!!" James whisper-yelled as he did the beheading sigh to Isabella, his body turned from John Jacob Astor.
"Can I help you, sir?" He asked. James slowly turned his head around and smiled. John Jacob Astor looked at James, including Madeleine Astor.
Isabella shoved James away then said. "My brother, James, is just VERY, and I mean VERY excited to see you; apparently, you're the richest person here?" John Jacob Astor nodded his head happily.
"That is quite true, little girl," He said.
James yanked Isabella away by the hair and whispered,
"Gaaaaaaaaaaaa…". He then shook his head a bit, his face turning

red, "I'm just so happy to see you...See you around Mr Astor!"
James said. John Jacob Astor shook hands with James, and then he
fainted on the floor; only in his head.
Immediately John Jacob and his wife disappeared inside a crowd of
wealthy people.

James stood there not exactly sure what to do next. He then realised
his family were probably eating, so he went away.
He got to the table and Daphne, Rosemary and Bridie were not
particularly happy with the idea of James coming back to eat with
them.
"I thought you would follow Mr Astor around for the whole eve-
ning!" laughed Daphne.
"Oh, shut up, Daphne! Hasn't your mother taught you anything
useful, but being a nincompoop?" James asked
"I would say the same thing to your mother!" Daphne replied
"Don't let me punch you down to 10th class,"
"I wish you can punch me now so I won't have to see your horrify-
ing face,"
"Sick burn!!" Rosemary blurted.
"Oh, so, second child wants to get involved; there's room for more;
let's start with you! Watch me get a lamppost, and I'll use it to hit
your head!"
"I'll punch you so hard that you'll make the earth rotate
10,000,000% faster than meant to!" Rosemary snapped.
"Can you all stop? You're showing bad influence to Anastasia and
Isabella!" Mother said.
"I'm not showing bad influence: I'm showing them what they
should do when an idiot forgets where they live!" He threw his
spoon in Daphne's mouth. "Ouuuuuuuuuuuuuuuuuuuuuch! That
hurts!!" A bit of blood dripped out of her mouth and she began to
cry. James cackled, choking on his water, "Make it stop!" He fell to
the floor laughing his head off, "Too funny to be true,"
"You're so mean!!" Rosemary snapped as she and her family hud-
dled around Daphne.
"Daphne, you had to be a bit stronger..." Edward said. Daphne
didn't say anything.
"Sorry..." Isabella, Father, Mother and Anastasia said.

"Hopefully that taught the fool not to mess with me, if that didn't work, I'll use an oar and thwack it in her face," James answered flatly. Daphne began to cry again and her family decided not to have their dinner with the Norfolk's.

73

CHAPTER 26

"James, I cannot believe you had the guts to hurt Daphne so badly that she's bleeding?! Do you know how painful that was?!" Father growled as he removed his waistcoat and looked at the time with his pocket watch.

"11:59…" He muttered. James didn't say anything as he buttoned up the shirt off his striped -blue pyjamas.

"You what?!" Alice asked.

"Removed your sister's canine," James muttered. Alice said nothing, but James saw a smile appearing.

"James, you have to handle yourself sometimes; actually, all the time!!" Mother said. She was looking at herself in the mirror and was drinking a glass of red, bitter wine. James sighed. He knew that was a little harsh and Daphne really didn't deserve it, but he didn't say anything because apparently, he was cold-hearted, which is quite unfortunate.

"We don't want you to cause any more trouble, or else…" Mother said, forgetting what James's punishment will be. Mother went into her room and closed the door as Father switched off the light from the parlour and went into his bedroom next door to Mother's. Alice went into her room and locked the door twice.

James groaned as he lay on the sofa, as he slowly closed his eyes pretending to sleep off.

Meanwhile, Isabella was having a sleepover with Anastasia. She was sleeping on the floor next to Anastasia. Isabella couldn't sleep, it was so hot! Like crazy hot! She stood up and switched off the radiator and went back to bed.

James was not asleep either; he didn't know what to do.

He was a bit hungry. But he didn't want to wake Alice up.

James mumbled to himself then opened the door and went for a walk. He wished he got his jacket because it was freezing like hell; even though hell is full of fire, but whatever.

Some dude was smoking and looking out in the water. He was a 3rd class passenger. He watched as James sat on a bench and stared at the floor. James began to think of his Titanic experience so far;

How he was so excited about going to America.
How he got to press the horn on Father's steering wheel.
How Isabella wasn't excited, but he told her to be.
How he met Daphne, and he hated her family.
How he messed up in front of Alice, and he cried.
How much of an idiot he was in front of Alice.
How he...
The man limped towards James, and James became scared.
"'Ello lad, wanna smog, I've got enough packets of cigarettes,"
The man said to James. He smelled like cow's milk, which James
despised. James awkwardly moved further away from the man on
the bench. The man shuffled closer to him so that James will be able
to smell him
"I don't know you, get lost!" James muttered as he put his hands on
his face and closed his eyes. The man put his hand on James's back,
and then he said, "Don't be like that, son, it's cool to smoke! You're
not a rich, selfish person…" The man said, "please come and live
with me!!" The man leaned in closer to James, and he kissed him on
the cheek.
"Ew, man!! Get a grip!!" James said.
"MARRY ME!!" The man pleaded. James shrieked at the top of his
lungs and ran away, screaming.

CHAPTER 27

The next day the Titanic stopped at Queenstown, Wales. Anastasia and Isabella were still asleep. Victoria rolled her eyes as she entered the room. Anastasia had to wake up because her cousins, aunt and uncle were here, so Anastasia had to wake up. She shook Isabella, but she didn't wake up.

"When are they gonna wake up?" Victoria sarcastically asked. Anastasia opened her eyes very slowly.

"Fantastic, Anastasia, you're awake, Maggie and Jasper are here, so you have to wake up," Victoria smiled. Anastasia smiled even more. She jumped up off the bed and fell on Isabella.

"Maggie and Jasper are here?!!! Oh goody, Victoria, they're the best cousins in the world!" beamed Anastasia.

"Do you mind not falling on me when you're excited, Anastasia?!" Isabella angrily grunted as she pulled herself up the floor. Anastasia didn't say anything as she jumped up and down.

"Go, Isabella, I need to get dressed, Maggie and Jasper are here!!!" Anastasia sneered with joy.

Isabella didn't say anything, instead she walked to her bedroom.

Everyone was dressed up. Alice was cleaning the place, and James was hitting lotta Spring on the floor. Isabella smacked James on the face.

"OW!!! WHAT WAS THAT FOOOORRRRRR?!!!!!" James asked as he whined like he was mentally annoying.

"Don't you dare touch, Lotta Spring!" Isabella threatened. Mother and Father walked out of the room. Mother wore a white and navy walking dress with a white picture hat; the pearl earrings and a navy pendant dangled every time she moved. Father was wearing a brown sack suit with his boater hat and black oxford shoes. He carried his black and golden cane.

James was wearing his Roll-Up II Panama fedora hat, his yacht suit and his golden ring.

"I really don't know why you're wearing such a thing, James. It's not a normal combination," Father said in his 'concerned' voice. James hates it when people use their 'concerned' voice because he doesn't know how to make the sound, and the voice is always spoken to him.

"Goodness, Isabella! You need to start to dress up! Do you know what time it is? 12:00 am! Let me help you dress up!" Mother demanded. "You can go without us, James and Alfred,"
Father shrugged his shoulders. "Come on, sonny! An adventure awaits!" James rolled his eyes.
"Let me get my diabolo and my hoop and stick!" James said. He ran under Mother's bed and got his toys.
"You still play with those things, aren't you 15?" Father asked.
"I can play with whatever I want!" James said as Father closed the door.
"That's what you said when you wanted to ride a bike at the age of 7!" Father laughed, "Happy days…" He whispered as he stared into space.

As the two of them were walking, James bumped into Mr Anderson, also known as Maggie's father.
"Aren't you meant to say something when you hit someone?" Mr Anderson asked, expecting a sorry or an 'I didn't see you there.' He wore a green sack suite and looked willing to kill James, but his orange fringe made it impossible to see if he was angry or not. James didn't say anything. Mrs Anderson whispered to Mr Anderson that they should go and this man was showing a bad influence on Jasper and Maggie. Mrs Anderson scanned at James, and they walked away, as Jasper admired his diabolo. James noticed the way Jasper stared at his diabolo with awe, so James pulled him aside.
"Wanna see some sick tricks?" James asked. Jasper nodded his head quickly. James made his diabolo jump up and down, move side to side and spin it around for about 30. 33 seconds until Maggie said,
"Come on Jasper, we need to go," She grabbed him by the wrist as he told her, "I want a diabolo exactly like that."
"Maybe you'll get one, maybe you won't," Maggie whispered.

CHAPTER 28

"Mother, I don't want my hair in curls!!!" Isabella whined as Mother curled each and every part of her hair. Mother didn't say anything. Isabella hated wearing her sailor dress, she found it so rubbish.

"We're nearly done with you!" Mother smiled as she put a navy hat on Isabella's itchy hair.

"Let's go," Mother then said as she closed the door.

Isabella ran to Anastasia, who was surrounded by many people.

"What's going on here?" Isabella asked as she barged passed the people.

"These were the cousins that I was talking about," Anastasia pointed out. She went to the parlour and pulled Maggie and Jasper towards Isabella.

"Isabella, this is Maggie. Maggie this is Isabella," Anastasia said. Isabella stared at Maggie.

She had amber hair that was in french braids, she had lots of freckles all over her face like Mr Anderson. Her eyes were a mixture of blue and grey, which made a dark colour.

"Hello," Isabella muttered.

"Hi," Maggie whispered. Anastasia pushed Jasper in front of Maggie.

"And this is Jasper, he's 5 years old. Jasper, this is Isabella," Anastasia mentioned.

Jasper looked like the opposite of Maggie. He had brownish blonde hair and chestnut eyes like his mother.

"Hello," Isabella said. Jasper ran behind Maggie.

"He's a bit shy," Maggie muttered as she stroked his silky hair. Isabella didn't say anything.

"Is your actual name, Maggie?" Isabella asked after an awkward silence.

"Um, no," Maggie said as she carried Japer. "My name is actually Margret, but my mother decided to shorten my name. She said Maggie sounds less like a bad stepsister name."

"What a weird reason to shorten a name," Isabella said.

"I know, right?" Maggie smiled. Mr Anderson and Mother walked to the children.

"Looks like we're all bonding, huh?" Mr Anderson smiled.

"It's so interesting to watch how children bond!" Mother smiled too.

"It can also be very uncomfortable, too," Anastasia said.

"Well, we best be going, now Isabella, Mama needs a walk," Mother said.

"Where are you going?" Anastasia asked.

"We're going to have a walk in the decks, wanna come?" Mother asked. Anastasia nodded her head.

"Oh please can we go, Sir, please?" Maggie and Jasper pleaded. Mr Anderson nodded his head.

"I'll be inside, organising the room," Mrs Anderson said.

Isabella stared at them.

"Do you call your father, Sir?" She asked as some dude opened the doors for them.

"No," Maggie answered. "We only call him Sir when we're in public. He said it's a lot more formal,"

Isabella didn't say anything.

They walked to the deck (while Maggie carried Jasper) and saw many strangers strolling and smoking. It was not a pleasant smell to Jasper and Isabella.

"Now," Mother said, "Where's your bonkers father and brother?" Isabella shrugged her shoulders.

CHAPTER 29

"Is that your son and husband?" Mr Anderson asked. Father was playing with a stick and hoop, and James played with his diabolo. "Seems like they quite enjoy games." He said. James stopped playing with his diabolo and told Father that Mother and Isabella were outside.

They walked to Mother and Isabella.
"Ello, Ello,wello!" James said as he high fived Isabella and Mother.
"What's that meant to mean?" Isabella laughed.
"It means hello," James said. He then stared at Maggie and Jasper.
"I know you and you and you," James said, looking at Mr Anderson.
"Yeah, you're the son that bumped into me and didn't say sorry," Mr Anderson smiled.
"I already hate you," James rudely hissed.
"In that case...!" Mr Anderson was about to say something when Father interrupted.
"Anyways, my name is Alfred, and this is James, my son, he can be quite annoying," Father said.
"Well, that's funny because Seamus is my name and it's the Irish form of James!" Mr Anderson growled.
"WHY?!!!" James kneeled to the ground looking up at the sunny sky, "Seamus is quite an unfortunate don't know why you're named that," James said.
"If Seamus is the same name as James, then your name is unfortunate too," Mr Anderson said.
Jasper went and tapped Mr Anderson on the leg and said, "Stop arguing, Sir, it's a bit strange…" Jasper said. Mr Anderson felt quite awkward and stopped speaking to James. Instead, he talked to Father.
"Wanna play with my diabolo?" James asked.
"Oh, yes, sir!!" Jasper beamed.
"Please, call me James! I hate the word, Sir!" James said. He gave his diabolo to Jasper, and Jasper smiled. James walked to a deck chair and put his shades on, then sat down and stared precisely at the sun.

"I can do some sick tricks with James's diabolo!" Jasper said to Maggie.

"Well done, Jasper! Show us some tricks!" Maggie smiled. Jasper threw the diabolo up and down and did some tricks.

"That's so cool!!" Anastasia and Isabella shouted as the diabolo went up and down. Jasper threw it so high that it almost fell out of the boat, but Anastasia was at the rail, so she caught it.

"That was close!" Maggie said as she got the diabolo from Jasper and Anastasia.

"Let's give it back to Sir, shall we, Jasper?" Maggie suggested.

"His name is James, and he doesn't like to be called Sir," Jasper acquainted. Maggie shrugged her shoulders and told Jasper to give it to James. Jasper walked away.

"Do you know why I'm going to America?" Isabella asked. Maggie shrugged her shoulders.

"My father has a ballet and contemporary studio called Studio élégant de Ballet," Isabella said.

"I'm fantastic at classical ballet," Maggie claimed.

"Really? Bet you can't do a Grand Jeté!" Isabella instantly demanded.

"Fine, I can do that, and I'll show you!" Maggie said as she removed her shoes and her hat. She rolled up her skirt to the top part of her thighs and went in position. She leapt up, toes pointed and went up in the air and landed back down. Isabella began to clap.

"It wasn't my best, though. I didn't really stretch or anything," Maggie said, a little disappointed.

"Don't worry, you still did well," Isabella smiled.

"Why don't you try to do a Pas de Chat," Maggie said.

"Simple, so, so simple!" Isabella said. She removed her shoes and her heavy necklace and gave it to Anastasia.

"What are you doing?" Anastasia asked.

"A Pas de Chat," Isabella answered.

"Nice," Anastasia beamed. Isabella breathed deeply as she rolled up her skirt and tied her hair with Maggie's hair band.

Isabella hopped sideways, bending her knees and brought her legs up high in a diamond shape before she touched down a little way from the start of the leap. She did it about 10 times.

"Bravo Isabella, bravo!" Maggie applauded. Jasper came back and noticed how he didn't get to meet Anastasia's parents.

"Anastasia, why isn't mother and father here?" Jasper asked.

"My mother said she was tired of the way I behave for some reason, so now I am going to live with my father. For the rest of my life!" answered Anastasia as she hated her mother. "He moved to America a couple of years ago, so my mother is going to be alone."

The wind began to howl in a foreign language. Maggie started to think.

"Anastasia, I need your pocket watch," She said. Anastasia got her pocket watch under her head and gave it to Maggie.

"Half-past one, we've been out here for some time," Maggie silently muttered under the songs of the cold wind.

"You know what, I love the accent of the Irish people," James said out of nowhere. It shocked Jasper.

"Where did you come from?!!" Anastasia and Maggie questioned. He shrugged his shoulders.

"Anyway, the reason I adore the Irish accent is that it's so like, I can't really say it, but they always have, like some weird tune in their voice," James said as he spat into the water.

"Are you even relevant?" Maggie asked with her 'concerned' tone. James walked up to her and did his signature face, aka his unpleasant face.

"To be honest, Margaret, I am quite relevant if you ask me," James said as he sprayed all over her face.

CHAPTER 30

"Relevant enough to chip someone's tooth off, yes!" Daphne said as she and her tacky family walked to James.
"When you think you have enough annoying people in your life for one day, the most prominently annoying type of people come." James sighed.
"James, pleasant to see you-" Edward beamed full of joy, but James chatted over him.
"Daphne, what are you doing here, I thought breaking your canine will prevent you from speaking!" James rudely demanded. Daphne, Rosemary and Bridie both did the sassy 'oh my goodness!' looks and glared at James. Edward walked away to Father, Mr Anderson and Mother.

James did his unpleasant face and clicked at them in front of their faces. Jasper was giggling behind Maggie in her orange hair.
"Are you sassing me?!!" Daphne asked. James spat at them. They began shrieking like dolls, then they quickly ran away apart from Rosemary. She spat at James, and he spat back, but some yellow snot went on her face. That thankfully got her running.
"Headless chickens," James said as he stared into the distance as if he was in an ancient story that was passed down through a million generations.

"Wasn't that mean, James?" Maggie asked as her hair blustered in the wind. James scanned Maggie then responded, "What do you know about idiots? They don't deserve to be happy!"
"Are you included in that category?" Isabella wickedly laughed along with Anastasia, who was lying on the wooden floor.
"Shut up!" James hissed. He used Isabella's hat and whacked it on her head. Isabella used her silky black shoes and thrust it at James. But he caught it with his hands. He then walked to the side of the boat and hung the boot over the fast-moving water, only holding the strap.
"Mother is gonna kill you so give it back," Isabella quietly threatened. James dropped it and caught it with his other hand, laughing.

"GIVE IT BACK!! MUMMY, JAMES IS NOT GIVING ME MY SHOE!!!!" Isabella screamed at the top of her lungs. Anastasia covered her ears and rolled on the floor. Mother, Father and Mr Anderson came running to the shrieking Isabella and saw what was happening. Father pulled James with the ear away from the water. James was laughing as Isabella scowled at him.

"James is a coward…" she unkindly whispered into his ear. James flicked Isabella's forehead, and they began laughing. Mother sternly forced Isabella's feet into her shoe.

"We best be going," Father muttered as he looked at his walking stick.

"Agreed," Mother says flatly. She picked up Anastasia from the floor, and the family walked away. "Bye," Jasper and Maggie said. Anastasia and Isabella said bye.

CHAPTER 31

Night struck, and Mr Anderson knocked on the Norflook's door. "Heeloo, how can I help you?" Mother asked. She was wearing a blue and green dress with a blue organza that was wrapped around her. Father and James wore double-breasted tuxedos and James wore a white bow tie with his white gloves. Father wore a black bow tie.

"I was just wondering if Maggie and Jasper could stay here for the night?" Mr Anderson asked. The two children weren't looking at all happy. They noticed that Isabella and Anastasia weren't going and they stopped frowning.

"We are going to the dining room. But, you lot are staying here," said Mother.

"Not fair!!!!!" moaned Anastasia, Isabella, Maggie and Jasper.

"BUT you can stay up late," She answered.

Mother gave Isabella a paper of boundaries while they're gone:

- No staying in your parents' room or James's bed.
- No coming out of your room.
- No speaking to strangers.
- No answering the door even if we knock on it.
- No fighting.

"Have you read that?" asked Mother.

They gave her a nod.

"May I ask, who drew the unpleasant face?" Jasper asked.

James said it was him and made the same unpleasant face.

"Come on, then let's go," said Father looking at his watch.

"We don't wanna be late," added James in the background of the whole thing.

"Be a good girl, Maggie, be a good boy Jasper, bye now," Mr Anderson said in a worried tone. Maggie and Jasper didn't say anything.

They closed the door and left.

Inside, the four children sat there on the floor in total silence. Alice
was dead asleep, and the children didn't want to disturb her.
"What shall we do now?" questioned Jasper breaking the silence.
Maggie looked around, "I don't know, we could watch a movie?"
"Sounds like a good idea to me," mentioned Anastasia. Isabella got
out the TV and put it in a plug and switched it on.
 "Well get some snacks," othered Maggie and Jasper.
"Let's watch… A beautiful diamond," Isabella suggested.
Watching the movie was slightly the wrong idea.
They next did some drawing, but still, it wasn't interesting too.
"We should just go to bed," sighed Maggie. "there's no point stay-
ing up for no reason." they all agreed, and they went to bed.

Father closed the door, and Mr Anderson stated, "You know what I
love about Titanic?"
"What?" James asked, bluntly. Mr Anderson scrunched his long,
pointy nose at James's rudeness, but replied, "What I love about
Titanic is how friendly the stewards and maids are,"
James thought of Alice for a few seconds, but he said, "That's the
most boringest thing about Titanic,"

"James, boringest is not even a word!"Mr Anderson snapped.
"Well, according to me, boringest is, too, a word," James said back.
"Your son, Mr and Mrs Norflook, is the rudest, mannerless and
annoying person I know. Did you even raise him properly?" Mr
Anderson asked. Mrs Anderson said, "I don't know anyone as rude
as you!"
They had reached the dining saloon, and Father said, "I don't know
why James has quite the behaviour,"
"You do realise I'm still here?" James rhetorically asked.
"James, you have to learn how to behave like a true gentleman.
Being a rude fellow won't get you anywhere in life. You won't have
friends, no one will like you, and you'll never get married and have
children," Mr Anderson said.
James thought of Alice again, then snapped, "I'm not rude, I just
know how to deal with idiots like you. Now stop determining my

future!!!"
No one said anything as they found the Mantoos on a table.
"Good evening, Edward. Mr Anderson, this is Edward, Edward, Mr Anderson," Father said.
Mr Anderson and Edward shook hands.
"Hello, James!" Edward said with joy. James didn't reply. He was about to hug James, but he quickly moved away.
"Don't be like that, James, let me give you a hug," Edward insisted.
"No. I don't want to," James said a little louder.
From the corner of his eye, Rosemary glared at James. James glared back.
"Stop glaring at people, James, I hear that you have to do something," Edward smiled. It made James feel uncomfortable.
They walked out of the dining saloon and into the smoking lobby.
It was full of men smoking and talking rubbish
"James, you do know why you're here," Father said.
James nodded his head, "I have to smoke!" James was really scared.
"There's genuinely nothing to worry about, James. Smoking is one of the best things for a man to do," Edward said.
"I don't agree with you," James said.
"I understand, you're still a boy," Edward smiled. He went into his pocket and got out a cigar. He gave it to James and said, "Give it a try,"
"How do you work this thing?!" James said, looking around it.
Edward got out a lighter and gave it to James. He lighted it up on the other side of the cigar and put the other side in his mouth.
"Then what?!" James mouthed.
"Just fill your mouth up with smoke then blow it out," Edward said.
James looked at Father. Father shrugged his shoulders.
James filled his mouth up with smoke and threw it on the floor.
"I don't like it!!!" he hissed. He moved away from Edward.
"Well, at least you did Alice's dare," Father said.
"Alice told you to do it?!" Edward asked. James didn't reply.
"Anywho, we should go now. We only came here for James to smoke," Father said, "Do you intend on doing it again?!" Father asked. James angrily shook his head.
"I'll never smoke again. Edward and Father laughed. James didn't.
"So, you actually smoked?" Rosemary asked. James didn't answer.

"Okay, we'll be on our way," Mother and Father said.
They all said bye and they went back to their guest room.
Everyone was asleep when they came back.
"WE'RE HERE!!" Father shouted.
The children moaned as they all woke up.
"Who made that unnecessary noise?" Isabella whispered.
"It was your father, Isabella," Mother said as she walked into her room and closed the door.
"Why did you do that? We were quite clearly trying to sleep!" Anastasia hissed. Father didn't reply to that comment, and he went to Alice's door.
"Oh, Alice! James did your dare," Father said, knocking on the door.
"Don't wake her!!" James snapped, turning red. Alice unlocked her door. Her nightdress was cotton-white that had puffy sleeves and flower designs near her chest. Her gown reached up to her ankles. She looked a lot like a little girl.
"What dare?" she mumbled, rubbing her eye.
"Oh, remember, Alice, when you told James to smoke," Anastasia said, standing up.
"You told James to smoke?" Jasper and Maggie asked.
"Yeah, do you have a problem with that?!" James hissed.
"So you actually smoked? How was it?" Alice asked.
"It was horrible, and I'll never do it again," James said. He went into his suitcase and got out his green and white pyjamas set. He went into the bathroom and dressed in it.
"Alright, time to hit the hay once more, folks," Father said. He switched off the light as everyone said goodnight and Alice went back into her room.

An hour later that night, Isabella had a dream. It was about her on the ship, but she was an adult.
As she got into the boat, it started to suddenly move quickly. And a few hours later, the boat somehow began to flood. She could hardly hold her breath and slowly, feeling dazed, she drowned slowly and painfully.

"AAAAAAAAAAAAAAHHHHHHHHHHHH!" she screamed. She looked left and right feeling really hot. Everyone was deep asleep apart from James.
He jumped off the sofa with black bags under his eyes.
"Are you mental? It's night time!!!" James scowled. Alice rushed out of her room and asked James and Isabella, "Did anyone hear that scream?"
"I just had a nightmare, go away…" Isabella coughed as she drank some water. James and Alice didn't really know what to say.
"I'll go get some hot chocolate and cookies for the three of us," Alice said. James didn't want Alice to leave, but he said nothing.
As Alice closed the door, James said to Isabella, "Let me go and get Lotta Spring for you. Go stay outside on the deck for a little," Isabella got her duvet and walked to the promenade deck.
James came back with Lotta Spring. Isabella took Lotta Spring and sat on the floor, wrapping herself with the duvet. James sat next to her.
"What was your dream about?" he asked.
"Nothing for you to know about," She replied, looking down at her doll.
James moved closer to Isabella and told her, "You know what I found confusing?"
She shook her head.
"Remember when Father shouted?"
"Yeah,"
"Everyone woke up. But you screamed in some dream, but Alice and I only woke up," James said.
"You and Alice," Isabella giggled. James slapped his head then said, "Stop it,"
"I was only joking," Isabella insisted. Alice came into the promenade deck. James blushed and looked at the floor. Isabella giggled silently.
"I've got the stuff," Alice said, somewhat confused at Isabella's laughing.
"Thanks," Isabella said. Alice gave James and Isabella a mug of hot chocolate and each a plate of cookies.
"Do you like the taste?" Alice asked.
"I'm lovin' this," James and Isabella smiled.

CHAPTER 32

Morning struck hard.
 The sun shimmered all across Anastasia's face, slowly she opened her eyes.
"RISE AND SHINE!" Isabella screeched, shaking everyone up.
"Good morning," said Maggie, along with Jasper.
 But Anastasia was still tired.
"I want to sleep some more!" she mumbled, turning the other way.
"Well you can't," Isabella shouted, happily removing her tied hair.
"You can't force me to," she said, looking at the ceiling. Someone knocked on the door.
"I got it!" shouted Maggie. She ran to the door, unlocked it, and some dude was standing in front of them.
"Stranger…" Maggie whispered as she stepped back.
 He said, "If you don't mind, stop making so much noise."
"My father doesn't find it funny." The man tiredly walked away.

"Y'all, we need to wake up!!" James said, already in his sack suit.
"We're gonna have an adventure today!!" Father smiled as he jumped up and down.
"Why?" Jasper asked.
"Because we're gonna do fun stuff!" Mother smiled.
All the kids dressed up, and they were able to convince Anastasia to wake up properly.
Alice woke up. She folded her bed and looked out the window; all she could see was the navy colour under the blue sky with cotton clouds, like thick pollen.

"Good morning, everyone!" Alice cheered as she kicked open the door. James blushed and looked away, fiddling with his buttons.
"Say, why don't you come with us, you deserve a break," Father insisted. Alice smiled.
"Come now, dear, let me get you something that you would wear," Mother said.
After 5 minutes, Alice came out of the room with a wide brim floppy hat, a white blouse, a silky black skirt, a bracelet that said 'Alice', she had green earrings and a white lace parasol. Maggie,

Anastasia and Isabella stared in awe. So did James, who blushed so much, that he went out of their guest room and leaned on the wall outside the house.

"You look astonishing, Miss Alice," Jasper whispered as he fiddled with her parasol.

"Thank you, Jasper," she said as she smoothed Jasper's hair.

"Let's best be on our way," Father promptly said. Father forced everyone out of the door. James blushed as Alice walked past him.

"I like your face," James blurted out. "Oh, crap!!" James muttered. Alice laughed. James locked the door. He then did an aerial and a backflip until Father told him to stop.

"I'm just havin' fuuuuuuuuuuuuuuun!!" James grinned as he did a cartwheel. He then carried Isabella, and she had a piggyback ride all the way to the decks. Jasper and Anastasia ran behind James as if they were aeroplanes.

CHAPTER 33

Alice lay on a deck chair next to Mother as she looked at Father and Isabella feeding the seagulls.

"Adventure," Father said as he gave some bird seeds to Isabella. James rolled on the floor to Isabella. "I'm bored!!!" He yawned as he used his gloved hand to hit a seagull. SQUARK! SQUARK! The seagull screamed. It flew and never came back.

"Oh, James, come and feed some birds," Isabella said. She poured a sack of bird seeds on James. Then all the seagulls pecked James all over.

"Help me!! Birds are EATING FROM ME!!!!!!!!" James shrieked. Father shouted some unusual noises, and all the birds flew away, Leaving James shaken.

"ISABELLA!!!!!!!!!!!" James shouted. Isabella stepped back and ran behind Mother.

"Sorry, James," Father said. James sighed and lied on the floor. Alice walked to James on the floor.

"Are you okay, James?" Alice asked. James turned red and closed his eyes. Alice sat on the floor next to James, so did Father and Isabella.

"Why don't we play truth or dare," Father suggested.

"We're listening," Alice, Isabella and James said as they all sat in a circle with Father.

"Hmm; James I dare you to smoke!" Alice laughed. James started to cough as if a fly tip-toed into his mouth. He then blushed because she said his name.

"Oooooooooooooo!" Father and Isabella gasped.

"There's no way I'm smoking! I'm smoke-free!" James yelled.

"You gotta do it! It's a dare," Alice smiled as she crossed her arms. James thought of Alice's hair.

"How do you EVEN smoke?!" James questioned. They all shrugged their shoulders.

"Okay, let's just hope I won't die!!" James said 'cheerfully'.

"Keep in mind that you're still doing it," Alice smiled.

"I know," James mumbled, thinking of Alice's brown beautiful eyes.

"We'll go to the smoking lobby with Edward at about 7:50, then

you'll smoke, James. Who knew bonding with people who are half
your age could be so fun!!" Father grinned.
"Very fun indeed," Alice said
James, Isabella and Father laughed so loudly.
"Wow," Isabella said, "James your hair is so soft,"
"Why Isabella?!!" James asked.
"Let me feel," Father said. James's hair is so soft it feels like a cat's
fur. "Good God, your hair's on point!!"
"Let me try," Alice said. James blushed as he felt Alice's smooth
hands on his hair. He's never been touched by her.
"Good God..." James sighed lovingly.
"How do you keep your hair in such good condition?" Isabella
asked.
"I may be an idiot all the time. But I'm not an idiot when it comes
to hair," James said.

They went inside, down the grand staircase. James saw a statue of
a cherub holding a light aloft graced the middle railing. It wasn't
wearing any clothes.
"Isabella, what's that?" he asked, laughing. Isabella peered at the
statue.
"It's a cherub," she answered, "Couldn't you identify that?" she suspiciously asked. James shook his head. "I mean what it's wearing!"
Isabella looked at what the levitating statue was wearing. It was
only a sheet or something. She understood why James was laughing; it wasn't wearing much.
"You're quite immature!" Isabella stated, rolling her eyes.
"I know," he laughed, "I know,"

"Let's go to the Turkish bath, Alice, Mama needs a back massage,"
Mother said as she walked to the Turkish baths with Alice.
"Come on, children, let's go to the drawing and writing room. We
can make paper boats! Then use James's paint to paint them," Father smiled. All the kids were satisfied with the idea..
"Don't make them touch my art stuff!" he grumbled, but the five of
them were gone. Including Alice and Mother. James shrugged his
shoulders and went to the dining saloon.

CHAPTER 34

James came back to the guestroom thing about 25 minutes and 45 seconds later. His hands were all wrinkled. He decided that he should have a warm bubble bath and sleep on Mother's bed for as long as possible.

"Mama needs her beauty sleep!" James said, thinking of Mother since she always said that. He walked up to the lift and went up to D deck. He then took the stairs and walked to the family guestrooms. Thankfully, the children didn't make the biggest mess he had imagined with his stuff.

"Afternoon James. You see I didn't say good afternoon or bad afternoon," Father laughed.

James wasn't at all sure what that meant. "Don't use the bathroom, I'm gonna be there for some time." He locked the bathroom door.

Isabella and Anastasia both painted the titanic with one of James's papers. Father went to his study and said he had to do some illustrations of Studio élégant de Ballet et Contemporain.

"What colour will it be?" Isabella asked as she followed Father to his study.

 "Green for boys, purple and blue for girls," Father answered as he sat down.

"Will there be a uniform?"

"Yes," Father said as he began sketching the top of the building.

"Would there be a pianist?"

"Yes, Isabella,"

"Would the building be big?"

"You'll see it when we get to America,"

"Would you have to buy your own ballet shoes?"

"Yes, silly Isabella,"

"Who is gonna-" Isabella said, but Father said he was quite busy, so Isabella left him to be excused. Mr Anderson then arrived and said that he'll be taking Maggie and Jasper for tea. So they took their artworks and left. Anastasia and Isabella began cleaning the place before Alice would come.

"Mama's back!!" Mother smiled as Alice came' crawling' behind as she adjusted her floppy brim hat.

Mother looked at the bell and thought of calling the steward, so she rang the bell. The man came in two minutes and asked, "How may I help you on this fine day, Mam?" Mother smiled and replied, "May our family eat our dinner here? We're not particularly interested in doing it in public,"
The steward told Mother they would only be able to eat a limited amount of food and Mother said that would be fine.

Anastasia said she doesn't want to eat her dinner here, so she and Victoria were going to go to the dining saloon and eat there.
"See you tomorrow," Anastasia said as she walked off with Victoria.
"I'm out of the bathroom," James said. He was dressed in his pJ's, and he put his socks on. "Where's Alice?" James asked.
"She went to get our food. Why are you worried? You already miss her? Or is there some kind of relationship between the two of you?" Isabella asked. Father laughed and started eating popcorn out of nowhere
"I'LL KILL YOU!!!!" James screamed. He chased Isabella around the rooms and eventually grabbed and began to pull her hair super hard. "AAAAAAAAHHHHHH!!!!!" Isabella screamed. James sat on her from the back and reached for scissors on the table.
"NO!! NO!!" Isabella screamed, thinking that he'll stab her back, "STOP!! SORRY!! I WON'T TALK ABOUT ALICE, PLEASE, JAMES!!!!!" She screamed. Father was still laughing.
He cut the back of her hair all the way to her trapezius, and he ran with her hair under the bathroom sink cutting it more and raging with anger.
"Oh, dang! Somebody just got told," Father laughed.
Isabella stood up slowly, "What... did...he... do?" Isabella asked.
"You don't want to know..." Father said, suddenly serious.
"TELL ME!!!" Isabella screamed.
"Okay!! He cut the back of your hair..." Father said.
"He WHAT?! And you did nothing about it?!" Isabella asked.
Father nodded. Isabella screamed and dropped to the floor.
"MY LIFE IS OVER!!!" Isabella cried.
Mother came out running from her bedroom.
"What happened-OH LORD!!" Mother screamed.
"James ruined my LIFE!!" Isabella said.

James slammed the bathroom door shut.

"You should've been watching," Father told Mother.

"We'll have to cut your hair," Mother told Isabella.

"WHAT DID I DO TO DESERVE THIS??!" Isabella asked.

"You made fun of him about his crush, Alice!!" Father said, laughing. "I DON'T HAVE A CRUSH ON ALICE!!!" James shouted.

"If you say so," Father said.

After 30 minutes, Alice, the steward and other waiters came to put their food on the table. The family, apart from James, dressed nicely. Isabella's hair was cut up to her shoulders, and when James came out of the room, she glared at him.

"Say sorry to Isabella, James," Mother said as she drank some type of soup. James sighed very deeply, then said, "Isabella, sorry for cutting your hair. I was a bad brother, and you didn't deserve to get your hair cut. I was just very, very, very, very, very, very, very, very angry about what you said,"

"Sorry for annoying you all the time," Isabella muttered.

"At least you got a fine haircut," Father said, smiling.

Isabella and James shook their heads.

"I wouldn't want to speak about that," Isabella said.

"You can eat with us too, Alice," Mother said. Alice said thank you and sat next to Father.

James went into Father's room and played the violin in there for a while.

After 10 minutes, James came back into the parlour and sat next to Alice, away from Isabella.

"You're excellent at playing that violin, James," Alice said kindly. James began to blush and looked at the floor, "I'm not that good,"

"Yes, you are!!" Father said, "Who taught you?!"

"I don't know. I went to a shop five years ago and I got a violin, and I began to play," James said.

"Well, you're really gifted," Alice said.

"Wow!!" James whispered to himself, "But I'm not as good at cooking like Isabella,"

"You can make the Norflook special," Isabella said.

"I can't make muffins like you do," James said to Isabella. Isabella smiled. They finished eating their food, and since Anastasia is in the

dining saloon, Isabella had to sleep on her Mother's sofa.
After that, Mother tucked Isabella to bed.
"Goodnight, sleep tight, make sure your dreams stay bright," Mother whispered as she kissed Isabella's forehead. Isabella didn't know what that was all about, but later she fell into a drifty sleep.

CHAPTER 35

"James, wake up!" wailed Isabella, about to pull his hair.
James gently exposed his eyes to the rays of sunlight. "Huh... what
is it," James asked, feeling very tired. "Can't you see I'm sleeping?!" he grumbled, turning to the other side of the sofa.
"But Mother just said we're allowed to go to the squash court!"
Isabella said in a persuasive tone. James stood up as swiftly as he
could and went to the dresser and looked for a suitable outfit to
wear. James turned to Isabella, "Count me in!" He pushed Isabella
out of the room so he could change. Isabella wore an orange dress
with a white hat and white tights.
She slid on some orange shoes.

"Fantastic we're all awake!" Father smiled.
Mother didn't say anything as she put on her white jacket. James
came out of the bathroom and did some stretching around.
"I decided I would be staying up here today," informed Alice,
"Someone has to take these dishes to the kitchen."
James wished she could come with them, but he didn't reply.

They got to G deck and walked to the squash court. Only Father
and James wanted to play, so Mother and Isabella went to have
some breakfast. They walked to the dining saloon and ordered some
scones, cakes and tea. Isabella saw Anastasia sitting at a table alone,
eating her breakfast in silence.

"Anastasia, come, move and sit with us," called Isabella. Anastasia
shook her head and continued to eat her grapes. Instead, Isabella
and Mother moved to Anastasia's table, and she was happy all over
again.
"So, Anastasia, how was your night, if I may ask?" Mother asked as
she put the napkin on her lap. "It wasn't good, Mrs Norflook. The
music was putting me off, and all the chatter at once. And I vomited,
and Victoria said that I should retire to my bed, and she made me
have a bath, and I brushed my teeth, and I read my book, and it was
all the better because no one was talking and I was well alone. And

I went to sleep and dreamed of the day," Anastasia answered as she chewed her grape.

The waiter came back with a silver tray of scones, Chelsea buns, carrot cake and Shortbread, and tea. Anastasia asked if she could have her grapes refilled, this time with red grapes. The waiter said he'll come in a second and Anatasia said it had already passed a second and the man awkwardly stumbled away.

"Would you fancy some carrot cake, dear?" Mother asked Anastasia. She shook her head.

"I am not fond of the colour orange. I am quite a selective person, but I would fancy a Chelsea bun," Anastasia stated. Mother gave her a saucepan and a Chelsea bun, then Anastasia sank her teeth into the cinnamon flavour. Anastasia gave out a warm smile.

"Thank you, Mrs Norflook," She said. Isabella wanted to change her dress at Anastasia's comment.

The waiter came with her bowls of grapes. She didn't say thank you because he was a stranger, and strangers were not kind to Anastasia. After their breakfast, James and Father came back from the squash court.

"It was toons of fun!" Father said when Isabella asked him how the squash court was.

"Do you mean tons of fun?" James sarcastically asked.

They saw Jasper and Maggie walking past them.

"Jasper, Maggie, do you want to come and play with us?" Anastasia and Isabella asked.

The solemnly shook their heads. "We're going to Cafe Parasine with the family, so I'm very sorry," Maggie said. Isabella said okay, and they walked off.

CHAPTER 36

"You lot didn't go to Sunday mass," Anastasia said.

"Aye?! Sunday mass?!!" James, Isabella, Father and Mother both questioned as they all sat on the deck chair. Anastasia nodded her head.

"I hate mass, you have to stand up for so looooooooooooooooooooooo oooooooong, and you have to sit down for a shoooooooooooooooooo oooooooooooooooooooooooooooort time!!" James said as he tapped his feet on the floor.

"I don't mind, we can all pray in our heads, can't we?" Father asked.

They saw Mr and Mrs Anderson walking among the decks.

"Mr and Mrs Anderson, where's Jasper and Maggie?" Anastasia asked.

"I don't know," Mrs Anderson replied. "They were meant to meet at Cafe Parasine, but they never came!"

"Well, that's concerning," Mother and Father said in their 'concerned' tone.

"I know, right! But we shouldn't panic, we need to start looking for the two of them!" Mr Anderson replied, and the two adults dashed off.

"They lost their children," James laughed.

"Let's go have our lunch, papa's starving!!" Father said, and they walked to the dining saloon.

Isabella picked the menu and looked at what it said;

R.M.S "TITANIC."

April 14th, 1912

LUNCHEON.

Consomme Fermier

Cokie Leekie

Fillets of Brill

Egg L'Argenteuil

Chicken A La Maryland

Corned Beef, Vegetables, Dumplings

FROM THE GRILL.
Grilled Mutton Chops
Mashed, Fried, Baked Jacket Potatoes
Custard Pudding
Apple Meringue
Pastry

BUFFET.
Salmon Mayonnaise
Potted Shrimps
Norwegian Anchovies
Soused Herrings
Plain And Smoked Sardines
Roast Beef
Round of Spiced Beef
Veal & Ham Pie
Verginia & Cumberland Ham
Bologna Sausage
Brawn
Galantine of Chicken
Corned Ox tongue
Lettuce, Beetroot, Tomatoes

CHEESE.
Cheshire, Silton, Gorgonzola, Edam
Camembert, Rouqufort, St. Ivel
Cheddar

"Does this make sense?" Isabella muttered as she looked at the menu. She doesn't usually eat food like this. She mostly eats chicken and chips.

"Mother, what shall I eat?" She asked. Mother looked at the list, "Try Fillets of Brill, that's what, Father, James and I are ordering," Mother said. Isabella agreed.

Anastasia was ordering vegetables with Cheddar cubes.

The waiter came and said that their food will be ready in 30- 35 minutes. Mother said it was outrageous once the man left.

CHAPTER 37

"Where are we going?" questioned Jasper gripping his next to Maggie's arm. "Aren't we meant to go to Cafe Parasine?"

Maggie didn't respond; instead, she said, "We'll get there soon." They continued to go down the lift until the man told them they couldn't go any lower. They were in third class, and Jasper looked into someone's bedroom. He quickly ran to Maggie and said, "These people are sleeping in bunk beds!"

"Bunk beds? Well, that's unfortunate!" Maggie stated.

Maggie and Jasper were finally stopped by a hallway that said: CREW MEMBERS ONLY. They continued walking until they found a door and opened it; they saw something unimaginable. Inside the room were large cylinder tubes of fire and men were shoving in coal.

"God Almighty!!! We should leave NOW!!" Maggie said. They were about to leave, but a man shouted out of nowhere, "OIH?!" he was coming towards them. "WHAT ON EARTH ARE YOU LOT DOING DOWN HERE?!" The man looked grey and grimy; he had a ghostlike breath, and he smelt like smoke.

"Um.. we want to go to Cafe Parasine." spluttered Maggie due to the volume of smoke in the room. The man's tired silvery eyes began to open.

"Are you lot stupid?!" He was about to erupt with rage. "Does this look like the top of the boat?!" He shouted, but he wasn't louder than the noise of the funnels. They shook their heads.

"You guys are right. This is the very BOTTOM OF THE SHIP!!" There was a profound silence. The man left, and the children were still standing there.

"Let's punish you the old fashioned way," grumbled the man, getting a cane.

Maggie said quickly, "Can you punish us differently like um..." she looked around quickly. "Like making us push coal for some time?" she pleaded with him to say yes.

"I don't want to do that!" Thought Jasper.

He dropped the cane and thought for a while. "I guess so," She began to smile.

"But, you're doing it until we get to America," he said.

"WHAT?!!!!" Jasper and Maggie shouted.

"Or you can get slapped for the whole journey; your choice."

"I think we're pretty good shoving in coal," choked Maggie. Jasper frowned quickly.

The man left with the cane and came back with two messy-looking shovels.

"You lot ain't doin' it together, you know!" he said, pulling them by their ears.

The man put Jasper in front of a tube, "Start shoving," he said.

He put Maggie in front of a pipe too. "Start, shoving!" And Maggie did what she was told to do.

"YOU MEN AREN'T GETTING A BREAK UNTIL WE'RE IN AMERICA!!!!!!!!!!!!" Shouted the man as loud as a hurricane. It felt remarkably impossible to do so, so Maggie hoped that was just motivation.

CHAPTER 38

Mrs Anderson slammed her palms on the table; making the food splutter and the cutlery rattle.

"Are you good?" James asked.

"Where are my children?!" Maggie's mother shouted.

"Someone pushed them overboard." Mr Anderson wailed panickily.

"Come on, let's all just calm down-" said Mother until she got interrupted by Maggie's mother and father.

"EASY FOR YOU TO SAY! IT'S NOT YOUR CHILDREN WHO'RE MISSING!!!!!" They shrieked so loudly at Mother's face that she heard a ringing noise in her ears.

"They probably went missing because of that constant screaming," James said. Mrs Anderson lunged onto the table and tried to grab James. Father, Isabella, Mr Anderson and Mother tried to pull Mrs Anderson away from James. "I'll KILL YOU!!" she screamed. James and Anastasia started laughing.

"No, you won't!!" James laughed with Anastasia

Father was forced to get the Captain, Edward John Smith of the ship.

"Okay, so how do your kids look?" said the Captain.

Since Maggie's mother and father were busy with their cries, Anastasia was going to describe her. "Maggie had curly orange hair. Her eyes are a mixture of blue and green, and she is nine years old; like us." "Jasper is seven years old, and his hair is light brown straight; his eyes are a mixture of green and brown."

"If you lunatics don't find my children, I'll kill all of you!" she shouted beneath her sobbing voice.

"We will find them," said the Captain.

"There's no way I'm helping the idiots to find her children; mainly because they almost made me deaf!" Mother grumbled. "Why can't she check on her children like me; I'm even able to look after my daughter's friend. It comes to show how unprepared some mothers and fathers are." Mother mentioned, laughing. She didn't notice that Isabella and Anastasia were here; listening. The girls rolled their eyes and walked out of the room.

"I can't believe that Maggie and Jasper are missing," said Anastasia, checking around the first-class dining room.

"It's highly not likely for them to disappear and no one knows where they're at," added Isabella. When they went to the first-class lounge room, a lot of ladies were comforting Maggie's mother. "Don't worry dear, I'm sure they'll find your children soon," said one woman. "You're too worried, put your mind on something else," added another lady.

Alice came into the lounging room with lots of cupcakes looking sad and worried. "Here you are, madam," she said, handing her a cake.

"So lovely of you" added Maggie's mother to the maid.

"I feel so sorry for you," said a younger lady, giving her sweet. Once the lady left Maggie's mother wept, "Why do I deserve this?!"

"Why are you here, Alice," Isabella asked.

"I went upstairs from removing the plates, and she told me to get her cupcakes!"

Anastasia and Isabella quickly left the room and unexpectedly bumped into James.

"Are you sad that Maggie and Jasper are gone?" complained Anastasia.

"It's good that they're gone; I couldn't stand all these annoying children." he laughed. Isabella and Anastasia didn't find that amusing. "Your sweet Alice is angry, you should comfort her; maybe with a kiss!!" Isabella giggled. James threw her shoe out of the window and went away like nothing happened.

"Well, that's my shoe gone," Isabella sighed.

CHAPTER 39

Evening struck, and there was still no sign of the two missing children. Isabella and Anastasia began to give up looking for them; there wasn't any choice even though it's not really true.
"Do you think we'll EVER find them?" asked Anastasia lying still like a rock on her bed.
"I don't know," mumbled Isabella looking out the sea, "I don't know."

At the bottom of the boat, Jasper and Maggie were still shoving in coal. Maggie's hands were droopy and mucky. Her eyes were so weak; her sight was vivid. "When will this torture end?!" moaned Maggie. She stepped back and saw Jasper chucking in coal. The only light Maggie was able to see was the hot boiling fire, crackling in front of her. She sighed and continued doing her work. Thankfully the stupid man allowed Maggie and Jasper to have a break; "You lot are so far doing well." he had said to them. Jasper walked weakly towards Maggie.
"I'll never ask for directions again," Maggie sighed as she sat on the floor.
"You said it, sister," Jasper whispered as he leaned on Maggie.
"I want to go home,"
"We will eventually," Maggie said.
"Eventually," Jasper said.

"CHILDREN," greeted out, Father to Anastasia and Isabella, "Mother, recommended we all sleep together for the night." The children started to whine.
"Sleep in the same room, no way bruv!" James winged, poking his head into Anastasia's slightly smaller room.
"Tut, tut, tut. It wasn't me who voted on this absurd idea. She believes we should stay together; having an eye on anything unusual," he ended, walking out of the room.
The rest followed, ready to have an unfortunate night.
"You just gotta be kidding me!!" James said as he jumped rapidly on the sofa.

"Don't worry James, we don't want you to be kidnapped on the ship!" Mother said. Mother switched off the lights and slept on the floor. So did Anastasia, Father and Isabella.

"Whoa, what's going on here?" Alice asked. James began to blush, and he looked away into his duvet.

"We're sleeping together, this thing thinks it'll be a good idea to stay in the same room," James said.

"I'm just being safe," Mother said. James rolled his eyes.

"Goodnight, then," Alice said.

"Goodnight all," Anastasia said

*****

"Goodness, my legs feel wet." moaned Maggie.

"What do you mean?" asked a dude next to her. They both looked down and saw the water splashing in from the wall. Then the man began to shout that there was water and everyone started to leave through the exit.

"MOVE, MEN! MOVE!!" The man shouted as everyone quickly made their way out.

"Come on, Jasper! Let's hurry!" Maggie said as she grabbed hold of Jasper. The water wasn't going to stop, and it began to be harder to walk as the water went higher and higher. The doors were automatically going down. Maggie and Jasper held their breath as the door went lower. Thankfully they made it, but others, I'm not quite sure.

"No time to stop, lads." answered the man running as quickly as he could. They all ran down the third class hallway, and Jasper and Maggie showed no sign of stopping.

CHAPTER 40

BANG! BANG! BANG! Went to Norflook's guest room.
James fell off the sofa, and he crashed mostly on Isabella.
"You mind?!!" Isabella, Father and Mother whined.
"The door scared me!!" James said. Alice came out of her room.
"Who's knocking on the door?" she asked.
"Only God knows," James yawned. He walked to the door and
opened it. A tall, thin servant-crewman said, "Sir, can everyone
inside the room get up from their chambres, wear their warmest
clothes, wear their life jackets and get up to the decks, please?" And
the man left immediately. James quickly grabbed the man by his
arm. "Why?!"
"Err...emergency practice," the man lied. James looked at him suspiciously for a long time, then said okay.
 Father woke up properly and yawned, "What was the lunatic
talking about?"
"He said something about walking up to the decks and putting on
your life jackets or something," answered James.
Mother quickly realized what he actually said, "LIFE JACKETS?!
This is the FILTH the man wants me to wear!!" she pulled up the
life jacket, "Look at the horror; it's actually wearing Hell. Even God
won't come except that!! I'll rather die than wear God's enemy!!
The life jacket!!"
"I really don't care," James said tiredly.
"Maybe it's not an emergency practice, and probably the ship will
sink or something," Anastasia said as she stretched and stood up.
"THAT SOUNDS SO GOOD!!" James laughed.
"This is all a bad dream; there's no way this is completely true...
RIGHT?!" asked Isabella, hoping this is not real.
"I'm sorry Isabella, this is all true and we're going to die! We'll die
slowly, and we'll say help, but no one will come to help, or we'll
die because everywhere is too cold," said James.
He got his woolly jumper, the life jacket, his black boots and all the
hot stuff.
 Anastasia, Mother and Father did the same thing.
"Either way, I'll be the one who has a 0.00000000000000000001%
chance of dying if it turns out this ain't an emergency practice"

Isabella felt like killing herself right now. She rolled around drunkenly on the floor. Everyone stared at Isabella, sort of scared of her.
"This girl's got problems," James said to Anastasia.
 "For the first time, you are right," Anastasia said back.
Isabella quickly knocked herself out of all the panic in her head. she stood up and said, "No problem, just put on some warm clothes, how hard is that?"
She stared at her jumper and placed it on.
"Come on, let us go on the decks for further notice," suggested Father and everyone agreed.
"Or, we stay here and sleep; this all might be a misinterpretation," suggested Mother. "He said it was a practice."
Everyone thought for a while and approved apart from Isabella, but she didn't show it. Alice knew it wasn't right, but she said nothing.

After 30 minutes, James noticed that people are beginning to go to the decks all in life jackets. Everyone was still awake, so there was no difficulty telling them. "Mother, Father, it seems to be so that everyone is going to the decks; should we start going?"
Mother began to laugh, almost choking, "Of course not; they're probably just having a walk; didn't you and Father do it yesterday?"
James nodded and sat back on the sofa.
"But let me and James check out the stupid commotion," Father said. James didn't want to leave Alice, but he said okay.
"Are you all buckled up, James?" Father asked.
"Yeah, whatever," James said tiredly. He and Father left the room.
"Good, now the worst people in the room are gone. At least one good thing has happened so far," Isabella said.
"I hope they don't take too long to check what's up," Mother said.
"They probably found Edward, and they'll talk forever!!"Anastasia assumed.

Then Mother saw Maggie and Jasper running past their door.
"'Eh! I saw the Irish kids!" Mother said and ran to the door.
"IRISH KIDS!!!" Mother called out.
Maggie and Jasper immediately stopped from where they were run-

ning to. "Did you hear that?" Jasper asked. "I think it's the Diabolo guy's mother," They turned around and saw James.
"Irish kids come!!" Mother said. They ran back to the Norflook's door. "Who the hell is Irish kids?" Isabella asked.
Maggie and Jasper came back into the room, "Hello, Mrs Norflook," Maggie said. "Where have you lot been?" Mother asked.
"You don't want to know," Maggie said. Anastasia looked at their clothes. It was full of soot, and their hair was all wet, including their faces. Maggie stared at Isabella's short hair up to her shoulders.
"Why did you cut your hair, Isabella?" Maggie asked.
"You don't want to know," Isabella growled. Maggie stepped back.
"Anyway, you shouldn't be here!!" Maggie said, "Titanic is sinking! Jasper and I saw it with our own eyes! We have to leave now!!"

Mother, Isabella, Anastasia and Alice said nothing.
"So are you coming?!" Maggie asked. Then Anastasia took off, running. "Anastasia where are you going?!" Isabella asked. But Anastasia didn't stop. Alice was getting a little ticked off, so she walked away. "WAIT!! Alice, before you leave, get me a cup of cappuccino,"
"You're actually joking!!" Alice asked. Mother didn't look like she was joking.
"I'll be on my way," Alice sighed.

CHAPTER 41

Meanwhile, up in the decks, there was so much confusion. Everyone was running up and down and screaming all over the boat. "Whoah, Father, there really was an iceberg that hit the Titanic," mumbled James. He walked around the ship as people were screaming and crying. The band played their tunes as the Titanic was full of chaos.
"Didn't that man say it was only an emergency practice?" Father asked. James said nothing. They had both never seen anything like this before.

"Father, do you think we're going to die because I think I'm gonna die," James said. Father didn't listen to what he said.
"Lifeboat..." Father said, "let me find a lifeboat..."
"Father, should we go back for Mother and Isabella?" James asked. Father nodded. He grabbed James by the arm and put him behind where a lifeboat was getting loaded.
Father said, "Let's wait near a lifeboat so that they would find us,"
"Sounds like a 'smart' idea, Pops!" James sarcastically muttered.

"Now be a good boy and stay here, I'll get Mother, Isabella and Anastasia," Father said. James' eyes widened.
"Bruv, you want me to stay here? Will you remember what lifeboat I'm standing here on?" James asked.
"Then try your best and see me," Father said then he walked away.
"Good idea, Father. Leave me here so I can fend for myself!" James groaned.

CHAPTER 42

"There you are!" Father said as Mother and Isabella were looking for Anastasia. Maggie and Jasper were there too. They're out on the decks and it was freezing outside.

"So good you're still here!" Mother said.

"I thought you left without us!" Isabella smiled.

"I thought the same, too," Father said, laughing as he stared into space. Mother and Isabella both exchanged weird looks.

"Hey, where's Anastasia?" Father asked.

"We really don't know! We were looking for her, and now she's gone," Maggie said.

"'Eh! You lot were missing! How did you get back here?" Father asked.

"You don't want to know," Maggie said.

"Anastasia must've gone on a boat already," Father said.

"I doubt that theory," Isabella muttered as Father pushed them to where James was.

That time some more people were going into the boat. James saw Maggie's family go into a lifeboat next to James's and Jasper told him bye including Mr Anderson. "I didn't know it'll all end like this, lad," Mr Anderson said. But James told him to get lost. James even saw the Mantoos's family get on a lifeboat and Bridie noted that he deserved to die. James almost punched her into the water, but she fell into the boat.

"We're all going to die! My Father was going to do business in America and is this how you want him to end his career and MY life?!" James shouted as men nodded their heads.

"Sorry, Sir, but I'm going to die as well! So can we all be less selfish, and listen to the Captain's orders!!" shouted a crew-man.

"Why do we care about his orders when the Captain is quite obviously going to die?!" a man shouted from the back of the crowd.
Then the crewman shot his gun in the air and everyone sort of screamed. All the men looked up.
"Now... are you lot going to listen?!" he asked, feeling quite cool.
The men nodded in silence. Father went in front of the crowd with Mother. "Whoa!" Father shouted as he put his hands in the air when he saw the man with his gun.

Mother stared in horror. Another man instructed Mother to go in the lifeboat. So she did.
"Wait! what about Isabella- my daughter- and my family and Anastasia?!"
 Isabella came out of the crowd because a man was carrying her by the leg.
"There's a child!!" shouted the man as everyone gave them space as she was carried through.
"Stop touching my ankle!" Isabella struggled.
"I don't find this any fun as much as you do!!" The man shouted back.

They plunged her into Mother's arm, and Bridie said,
"They're coming with us?!"
"If we annoy you, you can just leave," Mother said. Bridie backed off and turned around.

"James, Father come in the boat, there's room," Isabella said.
"Sorry, Isabella, women and children first." Father sighed.
"Even though I'm a child!!" James shouted.
"To society, son, you're a man," Father said flatly. James sighed deeply and sat on the floor.
"We're going to die, Father," James whispered standing, but

Father didn't hear him.

"I'm here with the cappuccino!!" Alice panted. She bumped into James, and some of the cappuccino splashed on the floor.

"Sorry," Alice said.

James started to blush, "Where's your life jacket?" he asked, pretending that the cappuccino didn't burn a bit.

"I wasn't able to get one," Alice replied.

"You can take my life jacket," James said. He removed it off himself, and he put it on for Alice. Father smiled.

"What about you? You need a life jacket," Alice asked.

"It doesn't matter," James answered. He then gave her his jacket.

"I don't need your jacket," Alice said. James wanted to stroke her face, but he said, "It'll get cold." Alice said nothing, and she allowed him to put his warm jacket on her.

"See you soon," Alice said. James nodded. Alice went into the lifeboat and said to Mother, "Take your cappuccino,"

She forced the cup into Mother's hand.

"Thanks..." Mother said.

"One more hug," Isabella said to the man.

He stared at her as if he was going to explode.

"Go on then! Get out!!" He shouted.

Startled, Isabella and Mother came out of the boat. The whole family hugged each other for the last time.

 Mother sadly kissed Father and James.

"This might be the final time we all see each other..." James thought.

"I don't want to go! James and Father will die!" Isabella moaned. "Isabella we'll never forget you! Go into the boat and be a good girl." James said, and he carried her into the lifeboat. Mother hugged Isabella as the boat went down and down; their faces full of tears.

Father looked down at Isabella.

"This will be fun!" Father said positively to James. James

didn't answer. His eyes were full of tears that he couldn't see so well.

"Aren't you going to ask what I'm talking about?" Father asked, wiping the tears off James' cold face.

"What are you talking about?" James sarcastically asked.

"We jump into the water and swim in the lifeboat!" Father said.

"We're going to die! Didn't you see all those men die?!" James said worriedly.

"Let's pray to God then," Father said.

After a minute, Father said, "Let's jump in!"

James didn't say anything. He looked down and saw so many people dying. "I can't do it!" he said.

"Yeah, neither can I!" Father said.

"Oh, Golly! I'm going to die!" James wailed as he watched everyone screaming.

"We might as well leave; that was the last boat," Father sighed.

"LAST BOAT?! YOU GOTTA BE KIDDING ME?!" James moaned. Father didn't have the strength to say I'm adulting you. Father walked away as James crawled behind; literally.

Father heard someone screaming, and the person sounded very familiar.

"James, do you hear that?" Father asked. James shook his head.

"No, no, no; listen properly!" Father said. James tried to listen 'properly' then heard a cry behind a wheelbarrow.

"The cry's coming from here," James said. The two men crept to the wheelbarrow. They looked over it and saw Anastasia; she was crying. "Anastasia?!" Father asked.

"What are you still doing here?!" James shouted. She stopped crying, then asked, "Where's Isabella? Where's your family? Why's everyone dying?! What's going on?!"

CHAPTER 43

"Could we stop and wait for Anastasia, Father and James?" Isabella asked, crying.
"Oh, God!!" Daphne whined, "Can we just leave already??!!"
Everyone on the boat went quiet, "You do realise that there are people there, yes?" Alice asked.
"Of course, I do!!" Daphne said. Everyone was still silent.
"Fine, we're only waiting for that stupid Anastasia!!" Daphne moaned.

Isabella saw Anastasia, Father and James talking to each other, then Anastasia was gone.
Isabella stared at the Titanic, her breath puffing out air.
"What are they doing?" she asked.

But what was actually going on was that Anastasia and James were talking to each other about how to get off the ship.
"Where are you going now?!!" James whined as Anastasia saw a group of children behind a barrel all crying.
"Leave the girl to do what she needs to do," Father said.
"What's the matter? Why are you crying?!" Anastasia asked.
James and Father walked to the children.
"Our father is dead! And we don't know what to do!!" the oldest child said as she hugged her brother and sister.
"We can't leave you here though, you'll die," Father said, already catching up on what was going on.
"That's what we're planning to do- die." The boy said, and they all began to cry harder.
"What about your stupid mother?!" James asked, looking at another firework that blasted into the air.

"Our mother has already gone into the last lifeboat, and we came too late," the youngest girl wept.
"Well isn't that good for you!!" James thought.
James annoyingly stared at the blanket they were holding; it looked more like a bedsheet.
" You're looking at us so weirdly," the boy said in his 'concerned'

tone.

"Why can't you lot use this blanket and use it as a parachute and
parachute your way on the lifeboat smoothly. That lifeboat is still
waiting!" James said as they walked to the rail of the leaning boat
and saw the lifeboat still bobbing on the frozen water.
"What about you, James and Mr Norflook?" Anastasia asked.

Father sighed and said, "Just do it!" He knew that his life might
come to an end, so he let the children survive. "Go!" he said.
Anastasia grabbed the crying children on her waist and told them to
run.
"HOLD ON!" she shouted, and they jumped off the boat and started
falling from the sky. She got out of the bedsheet and used it as a
parachute, and they went up and slowly landed nicely on the life-
boat. The children ran as fast as they could to their mother on the
other side.
"ANASTASIA!" shouted Isabella, hugging her so tight.
"YOU'RE OKAY!" Anastasia said; their eyes were full of sad and
happy tears.
"Wow mega happy ending!! We've all succeeded! CAN WE
PLEASE LEAVE NOW?!!!" Rosemary screamed.
"Calm down," Alice said.
"Mother! that is the girl who saved us!!" The oldest girl said happi-
ly, pointing at Anastasia.
"It wasn't me; it was James's idea,"
"This might be the actual last time to have a connection with James
and Father," Mother cried. "My poor son and husband,"
"My poor older brother and father," Isabella muttered.
"That's what you lot get since James chipped my tooth!!" Daphne
said. "Just give it a rest, Daphne!!" Edward said.
The lifeboat started to drift away, like the family drifting apart.

CHAPTER 44

"Wait a minute...." Isabella said, "Why are there some men on this boat when it's women and children first?"

"Oh, because since we're rich, we were allowed to board the life-boat," Edward replied.

"WHAT?!! My father is a rich man," Isabella shouted.

"Do you think anyone cares?!" a man said.

"Maybe no one cares, but not as they don't care about you since you ain't one of the main characters in this story," Isabella slapped back with her mouth.

"OOOORRRRR!" Everyone shouted.

"You just got told!!" Daphne shouted. The man turned red with embarrassment, then looked away.

"By the way Isabella, what happened to your hair? It was just a few days ago when your hair was up to your waist now it's up to your shoulders!!!" Edward asked.

"You don't want to know," Isabella said.

"Oh, yes I do," Edward replied.

Isabella sighed then said, "I was annoying James, so he chased me around our guest room. James then threw me to the ground, got scissors and cut a chunk of the back of my hair off. He ran to the bathroom and cut my piece of hair into tiny bits in the toilet. So then my mother had to even my hair out; by cutting it up to my shoulders,"

"Well, I hope that taught you to never mess with my son," Edward said.

"James is not your son," Isabella cried.

"We're going to die!" James said as he went to a man playing the violin and asked sadly, "Why are you lot playing the music, you'll all die. All of us will die."

"We're doing this so we can set a mood, son. Where is your family?" the cello man asked James. "My Father is over here," he said flatly, "Me mum and sister are gone in a lifeboat to the unknown." and he and Father walked away.

"What do you want to do in the meantime, son?" Father whispered.

"Die…" James said "… I want to die,"

"Negative, James…" Father said.

He and Father walked past a crowd of people saying the prayers: Hail Mary, Our Father.

James didn't join them; he didn't want to pray with a bunch of strangers. Father and James stopped and sat on a deck chair. There were 5 minutes and 30 seconds of silence; except the noise in the background.

"I'm… just, so scared, Father! What are we gonna do?!" James said, cracking the no- talking moment. Father didn't say anything.

"Let's go to the stern; the ship is tilting more on our end," Father said after what seemed like 5 seconds.

"You said it, Bruv!" James said. They began to walk to the stern without talking.

Then the lights went off, and everyone began to scream and scramble about, including James.

"I can't see much!" he shouted, but he could still hear a mixture of prayers and music.

"Come on, Son!!" Father shouted, "The more we hurry, the less we'll worry!"

It was more challenging to go to the stern because it was so dark. Father made James get bumped into moving objects. "Careful, Father! Don't kill me!!" James would always say.

They finally got to the stern of the ship, and now the boat was up-
right. Father told James to go on the outside part of the rail.
"Do I HAVE to?!!!!" James whined. Father said that he'll throw
James off the ship, and James did as he was told. Father did the
same thing after him. Some minutes passed, and Father told James,
"We won't die, James! We'll meet Mother and Isabella once Car-
pathia arrives!"
"And when will that be?!" He asked.
"Four to three hours," Father whispered. James was about to fall
off the rail. "Thanks for the fact, pops!!" James sarcastically said.
Father took that as a compliment and said, "Thank you,"
"I was sarcastic!" James said.
"Oh," Father said. "It's hard to know if you're sarcastic, especially
when your voice is always sarcastic," Father laughed. James smiled
and rolled his eyes.

There was a girl in front of him clinging on the rail from the inside.
She looked like an Israeli, and her hair was long and black up to
her waist. She wore a lapis-blue nightdress and a life jacket. She
was about the age of Isabella, and she had freckles on her knuckles.
James continued to look at her, and the girl was beginning to look
concerned. James thought that this girl seemed somehow familiar.
"Why do you keep looking at me?" the girl asked. James didn't say
anything; he looked harder at the girl and realised that she was Dixie. Dixie is a family friend to James and Isabella. She's not exactly
best friends with Anastasia and Isabella; she's more of a backup
friend to them. Dixie's best friend is Susan, but Susan isn't part of
the story. One problem was that Dixie HATED James- like a lot. No
one knows why she always says skinny flower.
"Are you... Dixie?" he questioned.

Dixie's brown eyes widened.

"Who are you, and how do you know me?" Dixie demanded.

"Um… duh! I'm James; how can you not know that?!" James demanded back. Dixie was about to fall off the rail and slide down the ship, into the -2-degree water.

"You gotta be kidding me!!!" Dixie snarled. Father looked at Dixie. "DIXIE?! Daughter of Mr Abend?! Who knew you would come and die with us?! A pleasure to be here with you, little girl," Father beamed. Dixie wasn't exactly sure if that was a good thing, but she smiled at him anyway.

"But, I didn't see you in 1st class. Or did you just lock yourself away from the world?" James asked.

"No, I didn't lock myself away from the world! I was in second class…"

The Titanic was broken in half, and the bow of the ship disappeared into the water. The stern went splashing into the water, and many people died as the stern crashed on them. Everyone was screaming; including Father and James.

"What was that about…" Dixie muttered to Father as she went outside the rail. There was a second pause, then Father remembered what Dixie had asked.

"The ship broke in half,"

CHAPTER 45

Passengers and workers were all clinging for their lives, some though, slipped and fell into the water and drowned.

"Do you think we'll make it?!" Dixie asked James.

"I'm not so sure, Dixie…" James answered.

Five minutes passed, and the stern was upright and was now starting to go down.

"Now, children, start kicking once you touch the water and hold your breath once I say so," Father said. James and Dixie nodded, and the three of them all held each other's hand.

The ship was insanely going down. Once they were a couple of feet away from the water, Father told them to start kicking and hold in a significant amount of air.

The ship was entirely gone, but the screams were still there.

Dixie couldn't swim, but James sort of helped her by swimming to the top of the water and he flung her out. However, Father let go of James, and now he was in the middle of the sea.

James and Dixie gasped up and down for air.

"So cold!!" he shouted. But it didn't echo through the night because everyone was screaming, shouting and crying. Dixie began to look around and saw that Father wasn't in sight.

"I say, James, where on earth is Mr Norflook?" she asked, coughing out some water. James shook his head, and he shivered in the ocean.

"Does it look like I would know? He let go of my hand, now, let's find a place to stay.

"What about your father?"

"He's gone somewhere, he'll come back."

"Are you sure?"

"Maybe,"

James couldn't believe that he was somewhere in the middle of the sea. They found a long, full piece of wood floating around and they swam to it; Dixie climbed on the wood and sat down, staring at the panicking and dying people. James sat next to her.

"Now," he said, "Let's l-lookout for F-F-Father!"

"You mean your father," Dixie said.

"Help us!!!" passengers cried as they slowly sank into the cold icy water.

"Oh, my goodness…" James muttered as the Titanic was invisible. "I am going to die…" He laid on the wood then went straight up-right as the sky was full of stars.

"We're not going to die, James! Stop being silly," Dixie said, shivering because of the cold.

"Who are you? The future teller or something; you can't tell the future!" James snapped.

"But I'm the kind of person who believes, and has faith," Dixie snapped back.

Father wasn't to be seen for the first few minutes but then plunged out of the water onto the wood plank.

"Where d-did you c-come from?!!" Dixie and James shouted. Father coughed out water for 4 minutes and 30 seconds then said, "That was a good thick cough. Anyway, I saw you lot on the long bark, and I swam to you, then a fool used me as a float, and my head went up and down," Father said, moving his head up and down. "Then I rolled around and pushed the fine sir into the water and quickly swam under the surface, so he wouldn't see me," Father went on pause mode and didn't say anything.

"G-G-good strategy, bruv," James sarcastically acknowledged. Father continued to say nothing.

CHAPTER 46

The lifeboat was moving gently, and Anastasia was well asleep.
"Who would be sleeping at a time like this?" Daphne asked.
"Probably passed her bedtime…" Rosemary said. Her and Bridie
laughed quite loudly.
"Isn't it passed your bedtime too, Isabella," Bridie asked. Isabella
glared at Bridie then looked down on the floor. Who would want to
sleep at a time like this? James and Father might be nothing more
than food for the sharks. The worst part of this whole situation is
that everyone said it was grand and unsinkable; even Father. Maybe if everyone stopped trying to be EXTRA, then perhaps they
wouldn't find themselves screaming for some boat to come and save
them." "And Mother, what will we do when it turns out that Father
and James didn't make it?" Isabella whispered as Mother looked
down at her muff.

"They're not going to die Isabella; I need to think…" Mother
whispered as she looked out to the sea. To be honest, she didn't look
like she was thinking, Mother was frozen like a grey statue called
Depression and Despair by the artist named Negativity.
 Isabella sighed deeply to herself, and Anastasia woke up.

"Are we still on the boat?!!" Anastasia asked as she leaned on Isabella.
Isabella gave out a weak smile and said, "We'll go on the Carpathia
soon. For now, we have to sort of wait,"
Anastasia nodded and then moaned, "Oh, I'm so hungry, my tummy
hurts!!" Bridie looked at her as if she had problems.
"There's no food, Anastasia!" She shouted bitterly.
 Anastasia quickly hid behind Isabella and demanded, "Is she
looking at me, and if she's looking at me, tell her I said I want her
to stop!" Isabella said okay and looked at Bridie; she was freakishly
watching Anastasia's breath next to her smoking husband, Edward.
"If only the water weren't as rough as our minds…" Edward said as
he continued to spread his smoking diseases around the unknown
misty air.

"Anastasia said you should stop looking at her," Isabella said.

"What? Was she talking to me?" The youngest girl asked, her name was Hazle.

"Nope," the boy and the eldest girl answered; their names were Charlie and Opal.

"I was talking to Mrs Mantoos," Isabella said, "Stop looking at Anastasia,"

Bridie was about to snap at her to shut up, but Rosemary complained, "I concur on what that girl is saying, you always stare at Anastasia; as if she's your daughter!"

Edward sighed and said, "Here we go again,"

"You always talk about Isabella, Alice and James, as if we're the FORGOTTEN children!" Daphne shouted.

"Maybe because you are forgotten!" Mother whispered.

"Leave Father alone, Daphne," Alice grumbled, "It's not really a good time to complain,"

"I don't care what you have to say, favourite child!" Daphne said.

"Wait...Alice ain't the favourite child! James is!!" Rosemary shouted, "He's not even part of the family, and somehow he gets ALL the credit! All he does is speaks rubbish, and he somehow gets favoured!"

"Who said I like James?!" Bridie said.

"NO ONE DID!!" Rosemary and Daphne shouted.

"James does not speak rubbish; he's kind and hilarious! Unlike you; your family only speaks of favourites and competition!" Isabella said.

"As I said before, you're not our mother!" Daphne said.

"At least she's doing a better job," Alice muttered.

"Now you're a 100% James! Are you his brother now?" Bridie snapped. Alice looked away.

"Do you really talk like this to each other?" Opal asked.

"Opal, they're strangers, don't speak to them," her mother whispered as she stroked Hazel's hair.

"This is completely normal," Edward said to Opal.

"Keep in mind this ain't an open conversation!" Daphne shouted.

"Judging by how you're all shouting, it looks obvious that this is an open conversation," Hazel said. Daphne snarled and said, "Did you get a degree on being annoying?"

"I don't think you can get a degree on tha-" Hazel said, but Daphne interrupted her.

"That's not the point! Anyway, if you speak to us again, I'll crack you like a hazelnut!" Daphne threatened. Hazle screamed, then started to cry.

"And I thought I was James!" Alice said

"Do you know what confuses me?" Daphne said.

"She's at it again," Edward moaned.

"Why can't I be the favourite child?! I'm the best," Daphne claimed.

"Please explain," Alice said.

"Today is Sunday which means tomorrow is Monday and Yesterday was Saturday," Edward laughed.

"Is that relevant?" Daphne asked.

"Anyway, the reason I'm the best is because I'm so smart," Rosemary said. "Oh God," Alice whispered.

"You...are not smart!!" Daphne shouted.

"I'll slap you!" Rosemary shouted.

"CAN YOU SHUT UP?!!!" A lady shouted.

"Who are you?!" Daphne and Rosemary asked.

"I'm a person," she replied.

"Who do you think you are?!" Rosemary asked.

"A person!" she replied again

"Hey! I got a joke!" Isabella said, "What happens if you eat yeast and shoe polish? Every morning you'll rise and shine! Get it?!" Everyone nodded. "Wait, I don't get it," Bridie said.

"Want us to explain?" Alice asked.

"Just wait...I'll figure it out."

CHAPTER 47

The night was silent and there was no sign of the ship, Carpathia.
Frost grew into Father, James and Dixie's hair and nose, and their
lips were red as cold blood.
"I'm... cold, Sir," Dixie whispered as she shivered next to Father.
He didn't say anything. But he did manage to give Dixie his hat and
the frost on her black hair slowly melted.

"The sun isn't out yet..." James said as he looked at the ice on his
nose.
"We're not gonna make it," Dixie said as she leaned on James crying.
"Don't cry," James muttered.
"Why wouldn't I? We're somewhere in the middle of the ocean, and
everyone is dead, I'm going to die, and my parents will cry," Dixie
whispered; there were many tears on her face. Father stopped sing-
ing, his mouth was shaking, and he said, "Where're the lifeboats...
Aren't they're coming," James and Dixie shook their heads.

Then out of nowhere, a small lifeboat was sailing in the water,
with a man with a torch, shouting, "HELLO, IS ANYONE OUT
THERE?"
James and Father quickly sat up and said, "H-HELP US WE'RE
HERE!!" but they sounded like a fly. Dixie used her shoe and hit the
wood, and the men saw them.
The boat quickly moved to them as the dude struck his torch at their
faces.
"Oh, good, you're still alive! Come in the boat quickly! We're
so sorry for how long you waited and the sinking," another man
sighed.
"It wasn't your fault kind sir," Father whispered as they limped into
the boat. "Yes, it was!!" Dixie and James snarled bitterly.
They gave Father, James and Dixie each a blanket and they laid on
the floor.
James was glaring at Dixie.
"What do you want?! Stop looking at me!" she asked.
"About a minute ago, you said that we'll die; b-but n-n-now look at

us! We're being rowed to safety!" James said.

Dixie rolled her eyes then whispered, "D-Don't w-waste our m-moment; I w-want to s-sleep, and I s-shall n-not be d-disturbed." She closed her eyes and went to sleep like Father.

CHAPTER 48

The clouds moved away as the foggy sun came out of nowhere. Isabella woke up, realising she was still on the lifeboat and forgotten of Father and James; as if they were sitting right next to her. Mother was currently in her Depression and Despair mode, so Isabella didn't disturb her.

"What time is it, if I may ask?" Anastasia asked as she leaned on Isabella as if Isabella was a dying body. Isabella looked up and saw a ship steaming to them. It was Carpathia, the boat saver.

"It's time for us to board Carpathia," Isabella whispered as she shook Mother to observe the fantastic figure. Like Heaven crashing down from the sky. Mother switched off her Depression and Despair mode and managed to give out a warm smile.
"Hopefully, we'll be able to find James and Father," she said. Isabella gave Mother an unpleasant look. "What do you mean, hopefully?" Isabella thought, "Has Mother already given up hope?" Isabella really wanted to scream her thoughts at Mother's face. Still, Isabella knew that was rude, so she didn't say anything.

"NOW I GET THE JOKE!!" Bridie shouted. Everyone woke up so startled, "You were still figuring out the joke?!" Daphne asked. "I was thinking about it ALL night, and now I GET IT!! Shoe polish will make you shine, and yeast will make you rise!! That was so difficult!!" Bridie laughed.
"It wasn't difficult to understand," Daphne said. Jasper woke up with a loud yawn.

"Come on, Maggie, wake up. The ship's here," Jasper said. Maggie didn't move. Mr Anderson looked worryingly at Maggie.
"Maggie, dear, it's time to wake up," Mrs Anderson said, her voice was loud. Maggie still didn't move. Her face was pale and her lips were sealed shut. Mr and Mrs Anderson began to cry.
"Mother, Father, why are you crying?" Jasper asked, his voice

cracking. But cracking. But the Carpathia stopped, and some men

The Carpathia stopped, and some men got out a looooooooooong ladder, and it looked a little strange. Mother, Isabella, Anastasia and others weakly climbed up the ladder, and they saw many Titanic passengers, taking everything in; the death, cries, the sinking and the cold. A man kindly took her to a lonely Depression and Despair bench.

"Thank you, Sir," Mother muttered as she sat down, thinking.
This part of the ship was steerage.
After some thinking, Mother demanded Anastasia and Isabella to find Father and James.
"It may seem boring, but we're doing this for our loved ones," she then looked at Anastasia who was scratching her left arm, then Mother added, "...And family friends."
They walked among the decks, and Isabella found it more like a search for water in a desert. 20 minutes passed, and James and Father were still anonymous.
"This is absurd Mother! Where could they be?!!" Isabella moaned.
"They're over there!!" Anastasia squealed as she quickly sprinted to James, Father and Dixie. Mother and Isabella scurried behind.
James and Father saw Anastasia, and they ran to her.
"Oh, good gracious me! I can't believe you're all still alive!" Mother shrieked as she kissed James and Father. There was a little pause, and James managed to blurt out.
"I thought we would die too!" No one has ever seen such an immense smile plastered on James's white, pale face. Everyone laughed at the sight.

Anastasia stared at Dixie who was looking out above the water, holding the rail, that wasn't leaning downwards, and the stern didn't poke in the sky.
"Who's that you lot were with her…" Isabella asked. Anastasia agreed. They walked behind her and Isabella tapped her on the shoulder. Dixie looked at them, and Anastasia and Isabella's socks popped out.
"DIXIE?!" they both exclaimed as they happily hugged her.

"Hey, I'm alive too!" Dixie smiled as she removed her hair out of her face and did jazz hands.

"I thought you wouldn't be coming at all; I bet Susan came too," Isabella said.

Dixie shook her head. "In fact, Susan said that her parents bought a farm in Scotland and now she'll be a barn girl. I asked her what barn girls do, and she said they make daisy chains, play in puddles and listen to their grandma's stories. She said that Susan is a perfect barn girl name so she'll be very excited. It sounded like a pile of rubbish and trashy idea, but I said nothing; I nodded my head instead,"

"Barn girls…" Anastasia said. Dixie saw her mother and father weeping about 20 meters away.

"I best be going," she said, "But let me give you something first, in case we never see each other again," Dixie removed her firefly hairpin and gave it to Anastasia.

"Thank's Dixie," she smiled. Then Dixie gave Isabella a paper, and for some reason it said:

Skinny
Flower

THE END